D0006919

J
CHR

Christopher, Matthew
F.

Tight end

$14.45

DATE			

Tight End

TIGHT END

MATT CHRISTOPHER

Little, Brown and Company

BOSTON   NEW YORK   TORONTO   LONDON

Library of Congress Cataloging in Publication Data

Christopher, Matthew F.
  Tight end.

  SUMMARY: A high school football player believes the harass-
ment he is experiencing on and off the field is due to his father's prison
record.
  [1. Football—Fiction. 2. Ex-convicts—Fiction]
I. Title.
PZ7.C458Ti   [Fic]   80–39744
ISBN 0–316–14017–1
ISBN 0–316–14054–6 (pbk.)

HC: 10 9 8 7
 PB: 10

MV

*Published simultaneously in Canada
by Little, Brown & Company (Canada) Limited*

PRINTED IN THE UNITED STATES OF AMERICA

To Scott

Tight End

CHAPTER•1

JAMES CORT, SR., came down the wide sidewalk holding a small, black suitcase in his left hand and a dark coat over his right arm. He was bareheaded, and wisps of dark hair whipped over his receding hairline from a light, Gulf of Mexico breeze. The September morning sun, shining directly into his face, made him squint.

"The best sight I've seen in two and a half years," Jim's mother said as they stood beside their car, waiting for him.

Two and a half years. It seemed like ten, thought Jim.

"He looks great, doesn't he?" whispered his sister, Peg.

"Great is right," Jim murmured.

Behind their father and the wire gate he had just come through loomed the high, gray walls of the prison from which he had just been released after having served time for embezzlement.

Jim's breath caught in his throat. His vision

blurred. He felt Peg's hand touch his, then clamp tightly around his fingers.

Mrs. Cort ran forward, her arms outstretched, her figure freed from the burden it had carried for over two years.

Her husband put down his suitcase and coat and took her in his arms. He was tall and lean, his skin pale. Once he had weighed close to a hundred and eighty pounds. Now he looked to be about one sixty. Jim, himself one sixty-two, five foot ten, and a sophomore in high school, could see that he resembled his father.

"Oh, Dad!" Peg said. Her green eyes misted. Then she, too, ran to meet her father, her long blond hair bouncing on her shoulders.

Jim watched as his father held both of them in his arms, his raw-boned face buried in their shoulders. Then he saw his father's eyes look up and meet his own.

The happy smile broadened. "Hi, son."

"Hi, Dad." In a minute Jim was beside his father, embracing him, hanging tightly on to him until the choked feeling in his throat wore off.

His father leaned back and looked at his bushy brown hair, his strong, athletic frame. "Hey, man, you're not only taller than I am, but you're better looking, too." He beamed at Peg. "Bet it's even-steven with the phone calls. Right?"

Jim shook his head. "Wrong. Seniors have more fun. She gets more than I do."

"Sure," Peg replied, her eyes flashing in the sunlight. "But they're mostly from girl friends."

She gave her head a saucy toss, letting her hair cascade in soft waves down her back.

"Don't worry," said Mrs. Cort to her husband. "You'll soon find out just which one keeps the hot line hot. Come on. We've got a long way to drive, and I'm not about to push that speedometer up past the fifty-five-mile-per-hour limit."

She hurried to the back of the car and unlocked the trunk. "Hon, put the suitcase in here," she advised.

Hon. It was a long time since Jim had heard that word of endearment pass between them.

His father laid the suitcase inside the trunk, slammed down the cover, and headed for the driver's side of the front seat. He and his wife met in front of the door, his hand on the door handle, hers on top of his.

"I'm driving, Jim," she said softly.

He smiled. "I know, sweet," he answered. "But won't you let me start out this beautiful day by being a bit chivalrous? I just want to open the door for you."

She beamed at him. "Of course."

He opened the door, waited for her to get in, then closed it.

Jim, already comfortable in the back seat, winked at his sister. She smiled back.

Mrs. Cort started the car as her husband opened

the door on the passenger side and got in. She pulled the shift lever to *D,* checked the traffic, and drove smoothly forward.

"Well!" Mr. Cort said as he laid his arm over the top of the seat and looked back at his children. "What's with you two? Hey, that's right! School has started, hasn't it? And now you're in your last year, Peg. Still playing the trumpet?"

"Oh, yes. I was lead trumpet last year, Dad, and Mr. Bush promised I'd be lead again this year."

"Good. Then on to college?"

She shrugged. "If I can make it."

"If you want to make it, you'll make it," he assured her. "What are your plans? Or is it too early to think about that?"

She smiled. "No. I've decided." She hesitated, glanced down, and smoothed a wrinkle in her dress. "I'm shooting for the moon, Dad."

"That's the only way. What's your target, sweetheart?"

"I'd like to be a research chemist."

"Ho-ho! That's my girl!" Her father reached back, took her hand, and squeezed it. "All the power to you, Peg."

Her face glowed. "Thanks, Dad."

Mr. Cort looked at Jim. "How about you, son? Are you playing in the school band, too?"

"No."

There was silence in the car for several seconds.

They all had their own thoughts, and Jim could guess what they were. While his father was serving a term in prison, money was tight for the other three in the family. His mother had found a job almost immediately after his father was imprisoned, but the job — she was a salesperson in a department store — didn't pay enough to allow for luxuries. And buying an instrument for Jim would have been a luxury, in Jim's opinion.

"Why not?" his father asked.

Jim shrugged. "Well, to tell the truth, Dad, I'm not really crazy about playing any kind of instrument."

Their eyes met. "I thought you said once you'd like to play the drums?"

"Yes. Well, maybe someday. I've still got a couple of years to go in high school to change my mind."

"Playing any sports?"

"Yes. Football."

His father glanced at his shoulders, his thighs. "You've got the build for either a backfield man or an end. I would guess end."

Jim smiled. "You're right. Tight end."

"Hey! Good!"

Jim had started last year in a running-back position, then had changed to end when Coach Dan Butler realized he could catch a ball better than he could run with it.

"Have you had any practice games yet?"

"Oh, sure. Matter of fact, we're playing our first league game Friday night."

His father grinned. "Nothing's going to keep me from seeing it," he said proudly.

For the next several minutes no one seemed to have a word to say, and Jim reflected sadly on the circumstance that had caused a complete change in their lives. His father had been an accountant for a car dealership in Port Lee. A strike in the automobile industry took place, affecting a lot of dealerships, including the one where his father worked. He was forced to take a big cut in pay. It was either that or get fired.

A month later Jim's mother suffered an attack and had to be rushed to the hospital for a gall bladder operation. Because their cash was scarce, the doctor agreed to be patient for his bill. The hospital wasn't as kind. Weeks passed. Bills began to mount. Jim's father started to inhabit some of Port Lee's bars. He never came home drunk, but Jim sometimes wondered if the amount of drink his father consumed could have influenced him to do what he had ultimately done: embezzled several thousand dollars from his employer.

He was apprehended at home one Saturday morning.

Jim could picture the scene in his mind as clearly as if he were looking at it now on a screen:

the knock on the door, the two men entering and introducing themselves as police investigators. They had his father's picture, and they asked him to go to the station for questioning. His father paled, got his hat, and left. The photo was somewhat blurred, but not enough to matter. The man in the picture was clearly James Cort, Sr.

What had helped the police trace him so quickly was the carelessness with which he had tried to cover up his crime. It was as if he wanted to get caught.

Dumb, Jim thought. A dumb, foolish move to get some quick money to help his family out of a growing debt. And look what happened. A two-and-a-half-year prison term, every minute of it undoubtedly filled with hurt and regret, and a sad, embarrassed, painful life for his wife, for Peg, and for Jim.

What now? Jim asked himself. What was their life going to be from now on?

They had dinner at home: Delmonico steak, whipped potatoes with gravy, honey-dipped carrots, creamed onions, corn on the cob, hot rolls, and pineapple turnover cake, Jim's father's favorite dessert.

"Good to be back in paradise, hon," he said to his wife, and reached over to touch her hand.

At eight o'clock, Ralph and Frieda Delaney and

their seventeen-year-old son, Barry, came over from next door with a large strawberry ice-cream cake. Barry was a junior in high school, a tall, ruggedly built boy who was vying for an end position on the school's football team. Although he was older, it was his first year, and Jim didn't think he was fast enough to compete with him or the others who were also fighting for the end spots.

There were awkward moments at first, as if the Delaneys didn't quite know what to say to the man they had once known before he went afoul of the law. But later, over coffee, the conversation turned to light topics and stayed that way, thanks to the talkativeness and resourcefulness of Mrs. Delaney.

The Delaneys accepted large pieces of the cake they had brought, and Mrs. Delaney immediately explained the problem she had in trying to bake a topsy-turvy cake. She found out, too late, that she had left out baking powder, so she had driven hurriedly to the bakery at Jacaranda Square. Once there she saw this scrumptuous-looking, calorie-loaded cake and bought it. She remembered that James loved cakes, and he couldn't possibly resist this one. She laughed and chattered on.

Almost without taking a sentence break, she started to tell about Ralph's coming home last night with a rip in his pants that had opened up during the third frame of his second bowling game. It had embarrassed her, because every time he leaned forward to roll the ball down the lane the rip got larger. She wanted him to go home and change his pants, but he refused.

"Go home and change my luck?" Ralph cut in, looking at her as if he couldn't understand her reasoning. "I had two strikes going into that frame, and finished up with a two-twenty score. I should let a little rip interfere?" He looked at Jim, Sr. "What would you have done, Jim? Would you have gone home and changed your pants?"

"Don't get James involved in this!" Mrs. Delaney exclaimed, striking her husband lightly on the arm. "It's your problem!"

Jim was glad they had showed up, but he was just as glad when they left at a quarter of ten.

The four of them retired to the living room and talked — about the children, and about Mrs. Cort's job — until ten-thirty, when the ringing of the telephone interrupted them. Peg went to the kitchen to answer it.

A moment later she was back. "Jim, it's for you," she said. A frown knitted her forehead.

Jim frowned, too. Who would be calling him at this time of the night? he wondered.

He rose from his chair, went to the kitchen, and picked up the phone. "Hello?"

"Jim Cort?" The voice sounded muffled.

"Speaking."

"Listen, we heard your father's out of prison. Why don't you get smart and quit football? Nobody will want to play with an ex-convict's son."

Jim stared at the receiver. "Who in heck is this?" he snapped.

The caller hung up.

CHAPTER•2

JIM STOOD, waiting for his heart to calm down. He tried to place the voice, but the muffled sound of it meant that the caller had probably used a cloth to disguise it.

Darn! Jim thought. Who would be so crummy and low enough to make a call like that?

He returned to the living room and plunked himself down on his chair. He avoided his mother's eyes, studying his left thumbnail as if there were something on it he had just noticed.

"Who was that?" Peg asked. "His voice sounded funny."

"It was Ed," Jim lied, and thought quickly for an explanation. "He wanted to know if I was up for the game tomorrow night."

"Wonder why he didn't tell me who he was?" Peg said.

"Did you ask him?"

"Yes. He just said 'a friend.' "

Jim got up and headed for the stairs. "Think I'll hit the sack," he said. "Good night, everybody. Real good to have you home, Dad."

"Thanks, son," his father said. "Darn good to be home."

"We'll be going up shortly, too," his mother said.

Jim went up the stairs, his gladness over his father's being home again suddenly clouded by the mysterious phone call.

He took a shower, brushed his teeth, and went to bed. He didn't fall asleep right away. The phone call stayed on his mind. He was trying to figure out whose face might be behind that disguised voice, and why the person wanted him to quit the team.

Why? Why should anyone want to make a call to him about his father that was going to gnaw at him till he didn't know when? Did he have an enemy he didn't know about?

It was late when he finally dropped off to sleep.

He started to get ready to head for Rams Stadium right after a light meal on Friday evening. While his father watched him put clean football socks and a couple of small towels into his duffel bag, Jim said, "Hope you'll see a good game, Dad."

"Me, too. But that's not important."

He paused, and Jim found his father's eyes focused on him with a strange awareness behind them.

"It's not bothering you that I'm going, is it, Jim?" his father asked quietly.

Jim's eyes widened. "Why, no, Dad. Why'd you say a dumb thing like that?"

His father smiled. "Sorry. But you look bothered. I just wanted to know."

"I just hope I'll do okay," Jim assured him. "I'm on the first string, but the season's early enough for the coach to shift me back a notch." He zipped up the bag, picked it up, and headed for the door. "See you at the game, Dad."

"You bet."

"We'll all be there rootin' for you," his mother broke in from the dining room. "Just come out of it in one piece."

"I plan to!"

Jim left by the front door, thinking about what his father had said, and about the phone call last night. The call had been bugging him most of the day. He had tried to read something cold or bitter in the eyes of the guys he had met and talked with during the day, but had gotten nowhere. He felt, though, that because the caller had mentioned football, he had to be a member of the team.

Jim paused in front of Barry's house and made a loud, sharp whistle through his teeth. Seconds later Barry came out of the front door, carrying his duffel bag.

"Hi," he said.

"How you doin'?" said Jim.

Barry came down the steps fast, and they walked up the street together. The boys had been friends since the Delaneys had moved into their home eight years ago. They had gotten into squabbles now and then, which sometimes had turned into fist fights. But the squabbles and the fights never lasted long. The boys would be sorry afterward, apologize to each other, and play again as if nothing had happened.

"Your father looks good," commented Barry. "Is he going to the game?"

Jim nodded. "He said that nothing's going to keep him from seeing it."

"Good go!"

At the school they went to the locker room, changed, and dressed. The Rams' uniforms were maroon with white trim. The helmets were white with the profile of a ram on their sides.

About a dozen players were in the locker room, suiting up. A flash of light lit up the room momentarily, and someone shouted, "Oh, knock it off, will you, Watkins? Why are you wasting that film in here, anyway?"

Jim looked up from tying his shoes and saw the

school photographer, Jerry Watkins, focusing his camera on a player putting on his shoulder pads.

"You do your job, I'll do mine," Jerry answered him. The room brightened briefly again as the automatic flash went off.

"What are you complaining about, Newton?" Ben Culligan, the team's one-hundred-and-eighty-five-pound nose guard, said. "This might be your only picture. You might not even get in the game."

The team responded with guffaws and sly remarks.

"Hey, Jim! Look this way a second."

Jim, his hand on the doorknob, turned and saw Jerry focusing the camera on him. He posed with a lukewarm smile.

"Come on. Let's have it. Show those teeth," Jerry coaxed.

Jim's smile broadened, and Jerry snapped the picture. "Thanks, old buddy," said Jerry. He grinned as he turned the lever for the next exposure. "If it comes out real super, I'll send it to *Sport Magazine.* And, look. Good luck out there."

"Thanks. I'll need it," Jim said.

A pleased grin spread over his face as he watched the slender, six-foot-one photographer move quickly, in spite of his slight limp, to another part of the room to get in position for another shot. Jerry's injury was the result of a motorbike accident that had happened two years ago at the Winternationals in Tallahassee. Jim's bike had hit a bump and crashed into Jerry's, leaving Jim with a smashed-up Kawasaki 125 cc, which was still in disrepair in his father's garage, and Jerry with a lame knee.

The accident ended Jerry's sports career, but it didn't keep him from being one of the best photographers Port Lee High School ever had. And his sports writing was as good as his pictures.

Jim chuckled as he considered the prospects of seeing his picture in *Sport Magazine.* That'll be the day, he told himself.

A girl came running toward him and Barry as they headed for the field.

"Oh, no," said Jim, cringing. "Where can I hide?"

Margo Anderson was in her maroon cheerleader's uniform. It was, she said, the closest she could get to wearing the football uniform of the Rams. After all, she could throw a football as well as some of the Rams players, punt almost as well, and wasn't bad as an open field runner. Jim had to concede that, because he had seen her perform in some pick-up touch games.

She stopped in front of Jim, smiling up at him from her five-foot-one height. "Hi!" She didn't seem to realize that Barry was there, too.

"Hi," Jim answered. "What're you doing out here?"

She got beside him. "I heard your dad came home. I just wanted to say I'm pleased for you."

"Thanks."

Neither he nor Barry slowed their pace, making her break into a fast trot to keep up with them.

"I also want to say something else."

He looked at her. She had short brown hair and dark brown eyes and wasn't bad looking. But how could he like a girl who said, herself, that she wished she were a boy? "Okay. Say it."

"I hope you score a couple touchdowns."

He stared at her.

She took off, darting ahead like a bird toward the gallery of cheerleaders sitting on a long bench in front of the south grandstand where the Rams' school band was slowly climbing up into the seats. "Crazy kid," he said.

He looked for Peg, caught sight of a flashing trumpet, and saw her getting ready to sit down.

"She's got her sights on you, Jim," said Barry.

"Who has?"

"Margo."

"Oh. Well, I wish I knew how to turn them somewhere else," Jim replied coolly.

"Why? Why don't you like her?"

Jim gazed at Barry. "Why should I? Girl jocks don't do much for me. Know what she told me once? She wishes she were a boy!"

Barry laughed. "She'll get over it."

"Maybe. Meanwhile, there are girls who are

glad they're girls. So why should I ignore them and pay attention to her?"

They reached a small crowd of Rams playing catch with footballs, and exchanged greetings. Jim wondered if most of them knew that his father had been released from prison. There was a piece about the release in the newspaper. Maybe some of them had read it and had broadcast the news to the others. The person who had made the phone call last night had certainly heard about it one way or another.

Jim got a sidelong glance and a quiet "Hi" from Pat Simmons, who was playing catch with a couple of guys. Pat, the Rams' left linebacker, was the son of the vice-president of the First National Bank of Port Lee, and nephew of the president of the company that Jim's father had robbed.

Jim's nerves tightened. He thought he could feel a change in the atmosphere when he came on the scene. Damn! They weren't going to ostracize him now just because they had been reminded of what his father had done, were they?

He got beside Randy Hardy, a defensive half-back, who was playing catch with Dale Francis, another halfback. "Hi, Rand," he said.

"Hi, Jim." Randy caught a spinner from Dale. He threw it back. Dale caught it and this time pitched it to Jim. Jim's tension eased as he continued to play catch with them.

The phone call continued to nag him, and he glanced at Pat. Pat was a big kid and had all the guts it took to make him the team's outstanding linebacker. He was tough on the field, and off. He wouldn't take anybody's lip. Jim had once seen him lay into a tough who was trying to bully a little seventh grader.

Pat surely couldn't have been the one who made that phone call last night.

What's wrong with me? Jim thought. I'm suspecting everyone. What I need to do is find who had a motive to make such a call.

Then he might be able to figure it all out.

The lights came on. Cheers exploded from the crowd, and the band struck up a chorus of "When the Saints Go Marching In."

Jim, waiting anxiously at his right-end position for the signal from the ref to start the game, felt tense and nervous. Somewhere in the stands were his parents. His mother came to all the games, but it was his father whose presence made a difference in tonight's game.

His dad had paid the penalty for his crime, but Jim knew that the stigma of it was going to remain with him. He would never forget it. He was going to be sorry the rest of his life for the stupid thing he had done. Jim knew this, and knew that he and Peg and his mother would have to live with it, too.

Whoever had called and harassed the family would see tonight that Jim was on the team for keeps, and that he wasn't ashamed of his father. They'd know better than to call again.

CHAPTER • 3

THE BULLDOGS' right corner man caught Mark Taylor's kick on the nine and carried it back to their thirty-four. They tried a line buck and gained three yards, then an off-tackle run that netted them a first down.

"Come on, guys," said Dick Ronovitz, the Rams' safetyman and defense captain. "Let's close those gaps. A truck could've gone through that hole."

The Bulldogs' fullback tried a line plunge and just about went over the line of scrimmage as Pat Simmons hit him with his full one hundred and eighty-four pounds.

"Second and nine," said the ref.

"Play in a little closer," Dick said to Pat and Steve. "Maybe we can make 'em fumble."

The Bulldogs' fullback tried a rush through left tackle and was thrown for a yard loss.

Dick grinned and slapped Ron Isaacs on the rump for the tackle. "Nice work, Ron."

The Bulldogs' quarterback went back on the next play, gripping the ball down near his knees. He faked a handoff to his left halfback, side-stepped Scott McDonald, the Rams' chunky left tackle, and heaved a pass toward his left side of the field.

Jim felt caught off-guard as he glanced quickly around for the man he was to keep his eyes on. He saw the player five yards up the field away from him. Putting on speed, he felt his shoes dig into the sod as he plunged after the player whom he was sure was to be the target for the quarterback's pass.

He saw the player look over his shoulder, then raise his hands to receive the throw. Jim surged ahead with galvanized speed. He closed the gap and leaped at the player as the ball dropped into his outstretched hands. He reached the guy, grabbed his waist, and hung on fiercely. He felt himself dragged a few feet, then had the man down on the ground, with himself on top.

Shouts rang out from the stands, and for a few seconds Jim wondered if he had hit the guy in time to cause an incomplete pass. When he looked closer at the receiver and saw the ball held tightly in his arms, dejection hit him.

"First down!" the ref yelled.

Jim got to his feet and glanced around at the player nearest him, Dick Ronovitz.

"Sorry, Dick."

"Yeah."

The disgusted look on Dick's face was unmistakable as he turned away, kicking at the sod.

Jim, his gaze on the ground, felt sure that the others would share Dick's feelings about the play. Well, he couldn't blame them. If he, Jim, had been on his toes, the Bulldogs' end would not have gotten away from him.

Damn! he thought, and promised himself that he wasn't going to let the Bulldog get away with that again.

The play had put the ball on the Rams' forty-one-yard line. The Bulldogs gained five yards on two consecutive rushes, then tried another pass. This time Jim made sure he covered his man like a tent.

But the guy was quick. He darted around like a bat. The pass went to him. He caught it on his fingertips, got his hands solidly on it, and Jim pulled him down almost where he stood.

But he had gained six yards and showed Jim a smile that revealed two rows of gleaming white teeth.

"I'm too fast for you, boy," he said cockily. "I'm like a bat. Didn't you notice?"

"Yeah. I noticed," Jim said.

It was the Bulldogs' first down on their thirty-yard line. Jim got to his feet and saw Pat talking to

Dick. Pat's back was turned to him. Chick Benson, the rover, was listening in.

Was Pat talking about him? Jim wondered. What could he be saying? I covered my man as well as I could. But the guy's quick. He'd give anyone a devil of a time trying to catch him.

The Bulldogs' quarterback rolled to the left on the next play and unleashed a long pass down the field to the right. No one was near the intended receiver, who was running clear toward the end zone. He caught the ball and breezed easily over the goal line for the touchdown.

The player was Fred Yates's man. But he was also Dick Ronovitz's, who was some ten yards away from the receiver when he had caught the ball.

Jim hated to see the Bulldogs draw first blood, but he felt good that it wasn't his man who had scored. At least he wasn't fully responsible for this touchdown.

The Bulldogs' fullback tried the point-after kick and made it good. Bulldogs 7; Rams 0.

Going back down the field, Jim heard the start of a conversation behind him that he thought was intended for him to hear.

"Our backfield defense stinks."

"You can say that again."

Jim turned around and found himself looking directly into Pat Simmons's hard, cold eyes.

"I suppose you guys are including me?" Jim snapped. "I had my man covered. The pass didn't go to him."

Pat's lips straightened into a thin line. "If the shoe fits, wear it, Cort."

Jim glared at him and looked away. Thinking back, Jim realized that since Jim was a sophomore and Pat a junior there had never been close ties between them. But the year's difference might not have been the real reason that their relationship wasn't on a more friendly basis. Jim now realized it was because Pat was related to the man who ran the company his father had stolen from.

A broad-minded person would know that a son was not responsible for his father's actions, Jim reflected. Maybe Pat wasn't broad-minded. He might feel that if Jim's father had committed a crime, Jim could not be trusted, either.

If Pat thought that way, could he have been the person who called on the phone last night? Jim asked himself.

From the Rams' side of the grandstand he heard the cheerleaders yell:

Sound off! T-E!
Sound off! A-M!
Sound off! T-E-A-M!
T-E! A-M!

The Rams are here to win, you're right!
The Rams will never give in, you're right!
Sound off! T-E!
Sound off! A-M!
Sound off! T-E-A-M! Yeah, Team!

The Bulldogs kicked off. Dick took the end-over-end, arching kick and ran it back to the Rams' forty-one-yard line before he was brought down.

"Power sweep to the left on three," said Chuck DeVal in the huddle.

The play called for Chuck to turn with the ball after he got it from the center, circle around the three backs behind him, and make a sweeping run around left end.

He gained eight yards on the play.

Then fullback Mark Taylor picked up a first down with a diving plunge through center for a four-yard gain.

They gained five more yards on two line rushes, then Chuck called for the twenty-eight roll-out option, on two.

"Get on your horse, Jim," he said.

Jim tensed. The play called for him to go out for a pass if a run by right halfback Tony Nichols wasn't going to work. He looked at the faces around him. Every pair of eyes was on him. He couldn't tell whether any of them doubted his ability to catch a pass, but it made no difference what they thought. The die was cast.

They broke out of the huddle and went to the line of scrimmage.

"Down! Hut! Hut!" Chuck barked.

Steve snapped the ball. Chuck took it, rolled back, handed it off to Tony. Tony headed for the right side of the line.

Suddenly two defensive Bulldogs broke through and came after him. He was forced to resort to the option.

Jim dodged his guard and sprinted down toward the right side of the field. Then he looked back, saw what had happened, and felt a sudden surge of tension. He was definitely a major part of the action now.

An instant later he saw Tony throw the ball, a slightly wobbling spiral that was arching high in his direction. Seeing that it was going over his head, he accelerated his speed to catch up with it.

Stretching out his hands, he caught the ball and started to pull it to him. It bounced out of his hands. Desperately he tried to grab it again. Instead, he knocked it aside. A Bulldog guard was there. He caught the ball, made a quick u-turn, and headed back up the field.

Jim, cursing his luck, reversed his direction and sped after the player. Ed Terragano got to him first and tackled him on the Bulldogs' thirty-one.

Jim watched Ed lift himself off the player and saw the scornful look on his face.

"Sorry," Jim said. "I should've had it."

"You *did* have it," Ed retorted hotly.

Someone bumped against Jim's shoulder. It was a hard thrust, and Jim was sure it was no accident. He turned and looked smack into Pat Simmons's steel-cold eyes.

"Too bad you missed that, Cort," Pat remarked. "Your father would've liked to see the kid turn into a hero."

"Yeah," said Steve Newton, coming up beside Pat. "Instead, the kid turns into the rear end of a —"

"Don't say it, Steve," Pat cut in. "You wouldn't want to hurt his feelings, would you?"

"No. I guess I wouldn't," Steve said.

Barry came into the game to replace Jim. As Jim reached the sideline he saw Jerry Watkins down on one knee, camera held close to his eye. Jim could hear the whirring sound of the camera as Jerry snapped a picture, and then another as Jim got closer to him.

Fine time to snap pictures, after I lose the ball to the enemy, Jim wanted to tell him. Or maybe I should say after I *gave* it to them.

He saw Coach Butler motioning to him. Jim ran to his side, unstrapped his helmet, and yanked it off.

"You all right?"

"Yeah, I'm okay."

Coach Butler was six one, and held his one-hundred-and-ninety-five-pound frame erect. A graduate of Florida State, he had been head coach of Port Lee High for six years and had accomplished an overall record of fifty wins, nine losses, and one tie. He didn't like losing. He didn't like a kid who didn't put out one-hundred percent.

His piercing blue eyes looked into Jim's mild brown ones. "You had that ball, then lost it."

"I know."

"Are you nervous out there?"

"No."

"You sure?"

Jim shrugged. "I don't know. Maybe a little."

The coach looked toward the field where the game had resumed with the Bulldogs in possession of the ball. His forehead creased with a heavy frown.

"You've got a lot on your mind, kid," he said. "And I can understand it. Take a seat on the bench. Cool your heels for a while."

Jim looked at him, then turned, found an empty spot on the bench next to one of the players, and sat down. He felt as if every eye in the stands was focused on him. His family's were, he was sure of that. They were probably looking at him with sympathy. He had caused the turnover. He was the target of attention.

The coach sent him in only once more. It was during the middle of the fourth quarter. He was part of the action in a pass play in which Chuck shot him a short pass, which he caught and carried for a four-yard gain.

He played until the two-minute rest period, then was replaced by Barry.

The Bulldogs won the game, 21–7.

CHAPTER•4

THERE WAS an after-game party at the school gymnasium. Jim had not expected to attend it, but Margo caught him in the corridor as he left the locker room and tried to coax him into staying. She was wearing blue jeans and a pink shirt that Jim was sure belonged to her brother.

"I hadn't planned on staying for the party," he told her. "My parents are waiting for me."

Her large eyes centered on him. "Tell them to come in," she suggested. "Parents are invited, too. I know Peg's staying. I saw her." She grabbed his arm. "Come on. I'll go out with you."

"Margo, I'm *not* staying," he said insistently. "And I don't think my parents want to stay, either."

"How do you know? Have you asked them?"

"No. But I'm —" He sighed. "You can be a pain, you know that?"

She smiled. "So can you. You know that?"

He tightened his lips, wondering how to answer that one.

"I know you like to dance. And you're good," she went on, pulling him toward the exit door that led to the parking lot. "And I know what's bothering you. That's why I think you should stay for the dance."

He finally yielded to her, letting her drag him to the door. He started to push it open, but she got to it before he did and opened it. He glared at her, shook his head, and stepped out into the cool night air. It refreshed him, and he sucked a couple of gulps of it into his lungs before he headed for the parking lot.

"So you think you know what's bothering me, do you?" he said, his eyes searching through the semidarkness for the familiar light-blue Chevrolet sedan.

Cars were parked all over the huge lot, but there weren't many. The Riverside High School bus was loading up in the lane between the school and the parking lot, and he waved at the players. They waved back.

"I think I do," Margo said. "Your father's out of prison. He was at the game. I saw him with your mother."

He glanced at her, a bitter look coming into his eyes. "So? What's my father got to do with it?"

She shrugged. "If my father just got out of

prison and came to watch me play, I think I'd feel pretty funny out there."

"Funny?"

"You know what I mean." She touched his hand. "You'll stay, won't you, Jim? Even if your parents won't? Please?"

They stopped walking and looked at each other. He saw she was a very attractive girl.

"Yeah," he said. "I guess I will."

Her cheeks glowed. "Thanks, Jim."

He found the car, and his parents waiting for him in it.

"Hi, Mrs. Cort. Hi, Mr. Cort," Margo greeted them, leaning down slightly to look at them in the front seat.

"Well, hi, Margo," Mrs. Cort said pleasantly. "Jim, I don't know whether you remember Margo Anderson or not. Her father ran for councilman a few years ago."

"Of course, I do," said Jim's father, his face dimly outlined in the half-darkness of the car. "How are you, young lady?"

"Just fine, thank you," Margo replied. "Why don't you come in and enjoy the party with us?" she went on hastily. "There are lots of other parents there."

Jim's parents smiled. "We'll take a rain check on it," Mr. Cort said.

"I'm staying," Jim said. "I'll go home with Peg."

"Okay. I'm coming back to pick her up at eleven-thirty," said his father. "See you and her then near the gym exit."

"Okay." Jim opened the rear door of the car, tossed his duffel bag onto the seat, then waved to his parents as they drove away.

"I think I know how he feels," Margo said as she and Jim headed back to the school.

"Maybe you do, and maybe you don't," Jim said.

He felt a sudden tightness in the pit of his stomach. Right now he didn't want to talk about his father.

Margo looked at him, the lights from the school reflecting in her eyes. "Okay. Maybe I don't. I suppose a dumb kid like me shouldn't have said a dumb thing like that."

"You're not dumb," Jim said. He sighed. "Anyway, I just don't like to talk about my father. I hope you understand."

"Of course."

They entered the school through the gymnasium exit, their ears bombarded immediately by the mixed sounds of voices and the rhythmic beat coming from the jukebox in the corner. Jim looked around until he spotted the long table with the cake and doughnuts and two large punch bowls on it and tapped Margo on the shoulder.

"Let's chow down on some goodies first," he said.

They walked along the side to avoid being bumped into by the bunch of dancing kids, and halfway to the table came face to face with Miss Delray, Jim's math teacher. She was a tall woman with black, frizzy hair and large, round-framed glasses.

"Well, hi, Jim! Hi, Margo!" she exclaimed, holding a glass of pink punch in one hand. "Tough game to lose, wasn't it, Jim?"

"Can't win 'em all," he said.

She glanced past his shoulder. "Didn't your parents come? This is for parents, too, you know. Parents and teachers, not only for the cheerleaders and the football team."

"They didn't care about it," replied Jim.

"Oh. Too bad." She smiled. "Heading for the goodies table? Don't let me stop you!"

They reached the table. Jim poured a ladle of punch into a paper cup for Margo, then one for himself. Then each picked up a piece of cake.

Suddenly Jerry Watkins emerged from the crowd, focused his camera on them, and snapped their picture. The flash caused stars to blink in front of Jim's eyes for a few moments.

"Good shot!" Jerry exclaimed. "Thanks, peoples!" He took a quick look around them, and his friendly smile faded. "Didn't your parents come, Jim?"

"No."

"Why not?"

"Mr. Cort said they'll take a rain check on it," Margo cut in.

"Oh." Jerry's right hand dropped to his belt buckle on which was a brass carving of a Texas steer head. Rubbing the shiny carving with his thumb, he sized Margo up, from her thick-soled shoes to her brown hair. "There's a guy standing like a lost sheep over by the jukebox. Have you seen him?"

Both Jim and Margo glanced toward the jukebox, emblazoned with sparkling colors, and saw Ed Terragano. He was alone and holding a paper cup. He was also looking directly at them, the expression on his face cheerless and cold. The instant their eyes met, he put the cup to his lips, tipped it up, then set it on top of the jukebox.

Jerry chuckled. "Methinks the lad is jealous. What do you think?"

Jim looked at Margo. "Jealous? Jealous about what?"

Margo's lips pursed. "Right. Jealous about what? I went to a couple of movies with him. We're friends. Just like Jim and I are friends." Her eyes smoldered for a second as she looked up at Jerry. "What're you trying to do, Watkins? Cause trouble?" She turned her back to him and dug her hands hard into the pockets of her jeans.

Jerry laughed. "See you around," he said to Jim, and left, his limp barely noticeable.

Margo turned back, grabbed Jim's hand, and pulled him out on the floor. "The bigmouth," she growled as they started to dance. "Why can't they let people just be friends? You know what I mean, Jim?"

"Sure. But maybe Ed doesn't."

She frowned. "What do you mean?"

Jim shrugged. "He probably thinks we're more than friends. How do I know?"

"That's silly," she said.

The music stopped. "You want to go over and ask him for a dance?" Jim suggested.

She stared at him, her mouth parting, and he suddenly got the feeling that he should not have said that.

"You want me to?" she asked.

He thought a moment. "No."

A smile flickered over her mouth. The music started again. She took his hand, squeezed it for just a moment, then held it lightly in hers. The feel of it made him think of a bird he had once held. He had wanted to put it against his cheek, feel its soft warmth.

They began dancing again. What's with us? he wanted to ask her. If you and I are just supposed to be friends and nothing more, why did you give me that dirty look when I asked you if you wanted to dance with Ed? And why should I be glad you didn't want to?

Suddenly he thought again of the phone call. If Ed had a crush on Margo and thought he was losing her to Jim, could he be mean enough to make that absurd phone call? Could he think that it would bother Jim so much that Jim would quit the team, and thereby cause Margo to lose interest in him?

How jealous can a guy get? How far would he go to hurt someone he was jealous of?

Margo's voice broke into Jim's thoughts. "Something bothering you?"

"What?"

"You're tense," she said. "And you're sweating. You okay?"

"Oh, sure. I'm fine." He forced a grin and loosened his shirt collar. "I'm sorry. I was thinking about something."

"I guess you were. You're not embarrassed being with me, are you?"

"No! What're you talking about?"

He tried to push the thought of Ed out of his mind. A few seconds later he saw a long-haired blond trying to get Ed to dance with her, and not having any luck. The more he thought about it, the more Jim started to be convinced that Ed Terragano was the person who had made that harassing phone call.

"Margo?"

"Yes?"

"Ed can't dance, can he?"

"I don't know. He says he can't."

"Is that why you wanted me to come with you?"

She stopped dancing and looked at him. "That's part of it, but not all of it," she said seriously.

"What's the rest of it?"

Her cheeks turned pink. "I'm not sure. I think I just like being with you. But I guess being with me seems to be bothering the heck out of you."

She let go of his hand, turned away, and headed briskly off the floor.

Jim followed her. "Margo! Where you going?"

"To get a drink!" she flung over her shoulder. "I'm thirsty!"

He followed her to the punch-bowl table. "I'm sorry," he said when he caught up with her. "I'll try to be more decent."

He picked up a paper cup and poured her punch, then poured a cup for himself.

He felt tense and extremely conspicuous.

Suddenly he felt a hand on his back. He turned and saw Peg smiling at him. Chuck DeVal was with her.

"Hi, brother," she said. "Hi, Margo. You two having a good time?"

"Yeah," he lied.

He barely looked at Chuck, whose black, wavy hair and dark features showed up his French-Italian ancestry. Chuck knew a smattering of both languages, and often amused the kids in his classes by rattling off something in either French or Italian. So far Jim hadn't learned more from him than *"Oui, oui," "Comment allez vous?"* and "ciao."

"Personally, I'm not so sure," Margo said.

Peg looked at her and then at Jim. Jim shrugged. "I think she means I'm not any better at dancing than I am at playing football," he said.

He drank the punch and set the empty cup on the table. "Come on," he said to Margo, grabbing her hand after she had drunk a little of her punch. "Let's get back out there."

They danced to a few more tunes, sat out a couple, and danced to a few more. It was a long evening, and he was glad when it was over.

He told Margo his parents would drive her home, but she said her mother was coming after her.

"Well, thanks for a good time," he said.

"Are you sure you mean that?" she asked him.

"I do mean it," he said. "Good night."

"Good night, Jim."

His father was waiting in the car for him and Peg when they went out to the parking lot at eleven-thirty.

Jim was having breakfast the next morning when the phone rang. His mother answered it. It was for him, she said.

He went to the phone, his nerves tightening. "Hello?"

The voice he heard was the same one he had heard before. He listened carefully, trying to recognize something in it that would give him a clue as to the identity of the caller.

"I saw your ex-con father after the game last night," the muffled voice said. The caller had probably wrapped a handkerchief over the mouth of the receiver. "He didn't look very proud. Maybe he wishes he were back behind bars."

Jim's grip tightened on the receiver. "Ed, is this you?" he snapped angrily. "Is it?"

The phone clicked as the caller hung up.

CHAPTER•5

"WHO WAS THAT?" his mother asked him, frowning. "I can usually recognize your friends' voices, but that one I couldn't. It sounded as if he had a mouthful of potatoes."

Jim tried to think quickly of one of his football teammates, other than Ed Terragano, someone he was sure his mother hardly knew. "It was Hardy," he said. "Randy Hardy. I guess he doesn't have good manners. He was talking with a mouthful of cereal."

He didn't know why he told her it was Hardy instead of Ed, except that he wasn't one-hundred percent sure it was Ed. If it were Ed, Jim wanted to let him know that he knew, and make Ed stop making the calls. He was sure that the minute Ed was convinced his identity was discovered, his perverted attempts at humor would stop.

As Jim headed for the living room, his mind still wrapped up on the call, his mother called to him,

"Jim! Aren't you going to finish your breakfast?"

"Oh, yeah. Sorry," he said.

He returned to the kitchen and sat back down in front of the eggs and toast he had left. The call had caused a lump to form in the pit of his stomach, but he finished his breakfast, put the plate and cup in the sink, and went to the living room.

His father was sitting in the leather lounging chair by the window, reading the morning paper. "Good morning, Dad."

Mr. Cort curled over a corner of the paper and looked over its edge at him. He was clean-shaven, looking younger than his forty years. "Good morning, son. How do you feel this morning?"

"Okay."

He sat on the divan, laid his head back, and stared at the ceiling. The thought of the phone calls began to gnaw at him. How could he prove it was Ed making them? That was the hundred-dollar question.

He tried to remember word by word what the caller had said. "I saw your ex-con father after the game last night. He didn't look proud to me. Maybe he wishes he were behind prison bars again." Or words to that effect.

Was Ed capable of saying those things, just because Margo had begun to show interest in him? Jim asked himself. Was he really that kind of guy?

"Something on your mind, son?"

The question from his father startled him.

"Nothing important," he said.

His father laid the paper aside, then folded his hands and stretched them out in front of him. "I noticed the look on your face last night when you answered the phone, and I see it again now. The expression's the same. I heard you tell your mother that it was Randy Hardy who called just now."

"It was." Jim felt his father's eyes probe his. He could remember that during his younger years he had tried to tell his father little harmless lies now and then to get out of a ticklish situation, but his father had always seen through them. He was afraid his father had seen through this lie, now.

Mr. Cort leaned over the side of his chair and looked out the window. "Isn't that Randy Hardy out there playing catch with Barry and another kid?"

Jim felt his stomach tighten. He got up and went to the window. His throat felt suddenly dry as he saw Randy on the street, catching a pass Barry had just thrown to him. "Yes," he said, embarrassed. "It is."

The next second his eyes widened as he saw the third kid who was playing catch with Randy and Barry. It was Ed Terragano!

Jim turned and looked at his father. He wet his lips. "Dad, how long have those guys been out there? Do you know?"

"No. I heard them yelling a couple of minutes ago. That was the first I saw them."

A couple of minutes ago. Then it could not have been Ed on the phone.

Jim returned to the divan and sat down heavily. His face was pale.

"You look as if you've seen a ghost," his father said. "What's going on? Whom or what did you see out there that's giving you that scared look?"

Jim took a deep breath, exhaled it, and told his father about the two phone calls.

"Hmm," his father murmured. "And you have no idea who made them?"

"Well, I thought it was Ed Terragano, but it can't be he if he's out there with Barry and Randy."

His father wanted to know why he had suspected Ed, and Jim told him. He felt foolish giving Margo's change of interest from Ed to him as Ed's possible motive, but his father didn't dwell on it.

"Now that you're sure it isn't Ed, who else is on your suspect list?" his father asked.

Jim mentioned Pat Simmons.

Mr. Cort gazed silently at him. Jim knew he didn't have to explain who Pat was. His father knew.

"Could be," he said. "But it's not likely."

"Why not?"

"Because he'd be too obvious a suspect."

"Maybe that's exactly why he would do a thing like that, Dad," Jim countered.

"Maybe. But you'd better make sure before you accuse him," reminded his father. "You wouldn't want to make the situation worse than it is." He cleared his throat. "Why should he, or anybody else, make such phone calls to *you*, though? What reason should anybody have to embarrass you by mentioning me in their calls?"

Jim shrugged. "I don't know, Dad. But one thing's for sure: it's bothering me so much that I'm only putting out fifty percent on the field instead of a hundred. You saw me last night. I should've had that pass. At times I only had half of my mind on the game. The other half was on what the guys were thinking of me."

His father frowned. "Because of me, you're trying to say. Because your father committed a crime and served time in prison."

Jim stared straight ahead. He found that suddenly he could not look directly into his father's eyes. He might break down and cry.

"No, Dad. No. I didn't mean that."

His father sighed. "Mean it or not, it's the truth. I've been a disgrace to you." There was suddenly pain in his eyes when Jim looked at him. "I've been repenting my stupid error ever since it happened. I don't know what got into me to do what I did. I must have been out of my mind. But I did it, and I can't undo it. I served my penalty, but I know that that doesn't make a bit of difference in certain people's eyes. They can't see — or they refuse to see — that I've paid my debt to society, that I regret with my whole heart what I've done."

Jim's heart was heavy. "I can see that, Dad. Mom and Peg can see it, too. I think a lot of people can see it."

"A lot. But not all," said his father. He picked up the paper. "I'm going job hunting Monday. If I can't find anything in the next week or two, I might consider going somewhere else."

Jim frowned. "You don't mean you'd move out of Port Lee, do you, Dad?"

"What else can we do? It wouldn't make sense for you, Peg, and your mother to live here while I live in another city where I happened to find a job, would it?"

Jim stared at his father. "We can't, Dad," he said seriously. "I have to find out who's making those phone calls."

A muscle twitched in his father's jaw. "I knew you were gutsy, son. I knew it all along."

A warm feeling came over him. He cleared his throat. "What kind of job are you looking for, Dad?" he asked.

"An accountant's job, like I had before. But I should do better now. I took an advanced course while I was gone these past two and a half years.

Some businessman in town should recognize that. Otherwise" — he smiled — "they might be losing a top-notch employee to another town."

Jim smiled at him. "I hope you find a job here in Port Lee, Dad," he said.

"I do, too, son," his father admitted.

Jim heard footsteps descending the stairs. Presently Peg and his mother came into the room, both wearing their light winter coats and hats.

"You two having a man-to-man talk?" Jim's mother asked, glancing from one to the other.

"Sort of," Jim said.

"Good," Peg chimed in. "That's proof that you should be glad we're not here to intervene. Come on, Mother. There's nothing like a man-to-man talk between a father and his son — in private."

They started toward the door, Peg leading the way. Jim stared curiously at his father. "Aren't you going with them, Dad? I thought you were going to buy some new clothes?"

"Your mother's going to get them for me." His father shrugged. "I'm not worried. She's done it before. She knows what I like."

Jim peered at him, wondering if that was the real reason why his father didn't want to go with them to shop, or whether it was because he might face embarrassment if he met someone he knew on the streets.

But he had attended the football game last

night, and he wasn't embarrassed then, Jim reminded himself. Had he attended it just because Jim was on the team, and felt that he was obligated to?

Jim sighed. He suspected it would be some time before he would really know the answers.

There was a knock on the front door. Jim answered it and found Barry standing there, his forehead beaded with sweat, his dark hair unkempt and matted.

"Hi, Jim," he said. "Feel like playing catch?"

"Yeah, sure."

He went out and played catch with the guys for about twenty minutes. Then Ed said he had to leave. During that time Ed had scarcely said two words to Jim, and Jim began to wonder about him again. Just how long had the guys been out here before his father had noticed them? he thought. The answer to that question could probably solve the all-important question: who was the person who had made those two harassing phone calls?

A few minutes later Randy left, too. Then Barry decided to call it quits. He was dying for a cold drink, he said.

"Want one, too?" he asked Jim.

"No, thanks," Jim said.

He wiped his sweat-beaded brow and headed for the garage to take a look at his damaged Kawasaki. He yearned to get it fixed and take it out for a spin, but he hadn't earned enough money yet to do so. Since his father had been away there had been a lot of other necessities that took higher priority.

He reached the narrow door next to the wide, orange-paneled garage door, and his hand froze on the knob as something on the door panel caught his attention. It was a drawing of a man in the black-and-white-striped clothes of a prisoner holding a large dish with a clock on it.

It took Jim only a few seconds to read the sickening meaning in it. The prisoner was serving time.

"Damn you — whoever you are!" Jim swore, and struck the drawing hard with his fist. Then he ripped it off the wall and started to tear it, when he suddenly stopped.

No. Save it, he told himself. Save the drawing. Maybe someone might recognize it, or recognize certain qualities about it that were characteristic of its artist. Maybe the artist, the screwball who had drawn it, was a student in Miss Talmadge's art class.

Jim folded the pieces, started to walk away with them, when something on the ground, next to the paved driveway, caught his eye. It was a yellow drawing pencil.

CHAPTER•6

HE PICKED IT UP and saw that the lead had been broken. Turning it carefully around between his thumb and forefinger he saw a name printed on it in bold type. PAT. There had been a last name on it, too, because its first letter was barely visible. But a part of it had been removed the last time the pencil was sharpened.

Jim peered closer at the letter. It looked like a *c*. He compared it with letters of the name PAT and saw that the *c* was smaller. The top half of the letter *S* would look like a *c*, he thought.

The name could have been Simmons. PAT SIM-MONS.

He felt an instant flood of elation. It was Pat Simmons who had drawn the picture! Pat who had made the calls! Yes! Pat, whose uncle had been hurt by what Jim's dad had done!

But what could he gain by wanting to hurt me? Jim asked himself. My father has paid for what he did. He'll keep on paying for it the rest of his life. Is Pat trying to get at him through me?

The thought weighed heavily on his mind. He considered telling his family about it — to relieve him of some of the burden — but he decided he'd wait till he saw Pat and got the matter cleared away.

He didn't see Pat till Monday at school. Tense, fighting to keep himself from hitting Pat first and asking questions later, Jim approached the burly, blond-haired junior in the cafeteria during lunch hour, held the pencil out to him, and asked, "Is this yours, Pat?"

Pat gazed at the pencil and frowned. "Why, yes. Where'd you get it?"

He reached for it, and Jim gave it to him. "Where do you think?"

"From my desk. Where else? It's the only yellow drawing pencil I've got."

He's either innocent or a terrific actor, thought Jim.

"Did you borrow it?" Pat asked. "Never mind. It's okay. But I usually like to know who borrows my things, if you know what I mean."

"I didn't borrow it," said Jim tersely. "I found it."

Pat's frown deepened. "Where?"

"By our garage, you bum. Near the door on

which you pinned your lousy drawing of my father."

Pat's face blanched. He sprang out of his chair and stood up so close to Jim that Jim could feel his breath.

"Just what are you talking about, man?" he demanded.

Jim's eyes narrowed.

"I don't know anything about any drawing," Pat went on angrily. "Anyway, if I did, you think I'd be dumb enough to leave a clue like my own pencil, with my name on it, close to it where you could find it? Don't be an idiot."

He snatched up his paper napkin, wiped his mouth, slammed the napkin back down on the table, and stamped away. Jim stared at his back, wondering whether to feel embarrassed or justified.

The football team was dismissed from school at three o'clock and was at the field, in uniform, by three-thirty. Jim hated going. The guys had hardly talked to him at the game Friday night. Why should they act differently toward him at practice? You would think it was he who had just been released from prison.

Apparently they believed that being the son of an ex-con was as close as you can get to being one yourself. Even though none of them said anything insulting to him, he thought he could sense their feelings by the way they looked at him. And one of them was the guilty rat who was calling him on the phone and had drawn that awful picture.

Coach Butler, with Hugh Gibson, his stocky assistant, standing beside him, conducted a conference first, bringing up the good and bad plays of last Friday night's game against the Bulldogs. He promised them that as soon as the movie film of the game was developed he'd show it to them. Nothing, he said, was better to point out mistakes, or successful plays, than watching the game on film.

Jim didn't care that the film wasn't ready for showing. He was fully aware of the big mistake he had made and didn't need to go through that experience again, even on film.

The team did the tiger dance — in which the first man knelt at five yards, the second man ran and jumped over him and knelt on hands and knees five yards beyond him, the third man ran and jumped over both players and knelt five yards farther on, and so on — until all the players were kneeling. Then Coach Butler had Chuck DeVal lead the squad in calisthenics, after which the team did the tiger roll. This consisted of groups of three men doing flying rolls over and under each other for about a minute.

Jim sensed both Pat Simmons and Ed Terragano avoiding him, and had a hard time trying to believe that neither of them was responsible for the malicious phone calls and the drawing he had found on the garage door.

Darn it, Jim thought bitterly, if neither one of them had done it, who had?

The backfield men began working on shoulder blocks with the sled, and the quarterbacks on their footwork and ball handling. Both Jim and Dick Ronovitz, ends on the offensive team, ran out for practice passes thrown by a back. Tony Nichols's throws to Jim were on the button, but Ed's were either overthrown, or too far on one side of Jim or the other.

"Come on!" Jim yelled at him disgustedly. But, if Ed heard him, his passes didn't improve.

During scrimmage, because there weren't enough players to make up two teams, some of the tackles who played both offense and defense in regular games now took their defensive positions. Pat Simmons, a right tackle on offense, played left linebacker on defense.

Chuck named a play in the huddle that called for Jim to run out to the right flat and buttonhook back for a pass. The pass was successful, and, although Jim was only supposed to run a few yards and then throw the ball back to the quarterback, he was suddenly tackled and thrown hard to the ground. A pain shot up his right elbow as the tackler, his arms tight around Jim's waist, rolled over with him and then flung Jim aside.

For a few seconds Jim saw fireflies. He waited till his head cleared, then rose to his elbow and gradually to his feet. He stared at the big kid walking away from him, a kid with the number 75 on his back. Pat Simmons.

"You okay?" Chuck asked him as he returned to the huddle.

"Yeah," Jim said, rubbing his aching elbow.

"He hit you pretty hard."

Jim glanced at Ed Terragano. "I guess there are a couple guys on the team who wish I wasn't on it. Maybe more."

Chuck frowned. "What gives you that idea?"

"Never mind. You're holding up practice." Jim didn't miss seeing Ed's cold stare before Chuck called the next play.

It was a draw with Mark Taylor, the fullback, taking the ball through right tackle. He picked up three yards.

Chuck called for two more running plays, then again a play that involved Jim: twenty-eight fly, on two.

They broke out of the huddle, went to the line of scrimmage, and Chuck began barking signals. "Hut one! Hut two!"

Steve Newton snapped the ball. Chuck took it and made a handoff to Ed. Ed started to run through the center of the line, then pitched it to

Mark. Mark cut to the right, the ball under his left arm. Then he stopped dead, grabbed the ball in his hand, looked for his receiver, and threw.

Jim, after faking a block on his guard, was running hard in a diagonal angle, from right to left, down the field. He saw Barry Delaney coming at him. Barry was playing left end now in place of Fred Yates, and was bearing down on Jim like a truck coming down a hill with its brakes broken loose.

Jim saw him, but he also saw the spiraling pass Mark had thrown. It was a beauty, a perfect spinner that was heading ahead of him and in the right direction.

He reached for it, grabbed it with his fingers, and started to pull it to him when Barry tackled him. The ball puffed out of his hands as Barry grabbed him around his waist, and then hit him with his shoulder. Barry was no giant, but at the speed he was traveling he felt like a two hundred pounder as he struck Jim and sent him flying to the ground.

He kept hanging on to Jim for several seconds after Jim was down before releasing him.

Jim got up, staring at him. "Hey, what're you trying to do, man?" he asked, frowning. "Squeeze my guts out?"

Barry looked at him. "Did I hurt you? I'm sorry."

"No, you didn't hurt me," said Jim. "But once

I'm down, I'm down. You don't have to hang on as if I'm going to get up and run again. Anyway, I missed that pass."

Barry looked surprised. He turned around and saw the ball lying there on the ground.

"I know you'd like a starting position at one of the ends, Barry," Jim said. "But I didn't think you'd try to kill me to get it."

"Drop it," said Barry indignantly. "I told you I'm sorry, didn't I?"

He grabbed up the ball, tossed it to Chuck, and started to trot back to the line of scrimmage. Jim shook his head, then followed him. It was the first exchange of unpleasant words he had had with Barry in a long time. He hoped it was the last.

"You had it in your hands, Cort!" Pat Simmons yelled at him as he approached the scrimmage line. "Wash off that butter, why don't you?"

"Knock it off," Chuck ordered. He met Jim's eyes. "What's the matter with you guys? Something happen between you two some of us don't know about?"

Jim didn't answer.

"Oh, Pat's got a bug up his nose," said Tony Nichols. "His uncle's the president of the firm in Searly that Jim's father robbed." He paused, and shrugged. "Anyway, I think that's why he's giving Jim a hard time."

Chuck frowned. "Jim, shall I tell Coach?" he asked.

"No. It'll straighten out."

"Hey! Come on, you guys!" Coach Gibson yelled from the other side of the scrimmage line. "Shake it up, will you?"

"Let's go," said Chuck. "Forty-five, on three."

It was a through-tackle run, with Tony carrying the ball. Jim, dodging Barry, sprang toward the right flat as if he were going out for a long pass. He stopped running when he saw that Tony had made the play through the line, gaining about five yards.

"Hold it, Barry," Jim said, raising a hand as Barry bore down on him. "The play's over."

Barry stopped running, his cleats digging into the sod, and turned. His shoulders slumped as he ambled back to the line of scrimmage.

Jim shook his head. Were Barry's brains ever going to catch up with his size? he wondered.

The practice ended with a run around the field, then a one-hundred-yard sprint, after which the team headed for a much welcomed, cool, refreshing shower.

As Jim neared the gymnasium door, he saw Jerry Watkins breezing around the corner on his motorbike. It was the same one he had cracked up in the Winternationals.

"Hi," said Jerry, pulling up beside Jim and cutting the engine to idle. "How did practice go?"

"Okay."

Jim looked at the polished black, single-cylindered Honda under Jerry and felt a twinge of nostalgia. Someday, maybe, he'd get his Kawasaki fixed up and start riding it again. "Hey, man, this looks just as sharp as the day you bought it."

Jerry smiled thinly and gave the throttle a short twist. "Yeah," he said. "They can fix machines good as new."

Suddenly a thought popped into Jim's mind. "Jerry, you get around school more than most of us do," he said, glancing around to make sure no one else was within hearing distance. "Do you know anyone on our football team who is a good artist? I mean real good."

Jerry frowned at him. "I might. Why?"

"I'd like to know."

Jerry shrugged. "Okay. I know one."

"Who?"

"Pat Simmons."

Him again!

"Pat?" said Jim. His heart skipped a beat. Pat had denied knowing about the drawing. But, if Jim could prove it was his, then he could prove Pat was lying.

"Jerry, do you think that you're familiar enough with his work to recognize it if you didn't know beforehand that he had drawn it?"

"I don't know. Why?" he asked again curiously. "What's this all about?"

Jim's mind was spinning in high gear. "I'll explain later. Will you have time to ride over to my place as soon as I get ready? I'd like to show you something."

"Sure."

Jim smiled. "Thanks. See you in a few minutes."

CHAPTER • 7

JIM COULD hardly wait to get home to show Jerry the drawing. If Jerry could be sure that it was done by Pat Simmons, then Pat had lied. Even though Pat had not put his name on the drawing, Jerry's testimony, and Pat's pencil found near the drawing, should be enough evidence in Jim's favor to confront Pat and make him stop the telephone calls. Such calls were against the law. Certainly Pat knew that. And if he knew what was good for him, he would stop making them.

Jerry drove his bike slowly alongside Jim while Jim trotted at a steady pace between him and the curb. Jim was also anxious to know if his father had found a job, but that was something he didn't care to mention to Jerry. So far, he'd managed to keep his father out of any conversation he had with people at school.

He finally reached home, told Jerry he'd be right out with the drawing, and went into the house. He said a hurried hello to his mother and Peg, who were in the kitchen getting dinner ready, and ran up to his room for the drawing. He kept it folded as he rushed past them and out the kitchen door.

Unfolding it before Jerry, Jim said, "Well, can you tell who did this?"

Jerry took it from him. For a moment he sat on his motorbike, studying the drawing in silence. Finally he said, "It's good, but it's not Pat's. Pat uses stronger lines. And his shading's darker. Take a look at some of his work in school. You'll see what I mean."

He handed it back to Jim. "Where'd you find it?" he asked.

"Stuck on our garage door." Jim refolded the drawing. "Do me a favor, will you? Don't mention this drawing to Pat, or anyone else. If you happen to hear who did it, though —"

"I'll let you know," Jerry cut in. He turned the grip on the handlebar. The engine roared. "See you, Jim."

"Thanks, Jerry."

He watched Jerry ride off, then walked into the house. Peg glanced at the folded drawing he tried to keep hidden from view, and stepped in front of him.

"What have you got there?" she wanted to know.

"Don't get nosy. It's just a drawing." He put it behind him and tried to pass by her.

She grabbed his arm and met his eyes. "I know about those phone calls. Dad told Mom, and Mom told me."

Jim shot a look at his mother and met her mild, understanding eyes.

"Does this drawing have some connection with those calls?" Peg inquired.

Jim heaved a sigh and unfolded the drawing. His mother came forward, and both she and Peg looked at it.

"My Lord, who did that?" Mrs. Cort exclaimed.

Jim refolded the drawing. "That's what I'm trying to find out," he said gravely. "I found it stuck to our garage door last Saturday afternoon. Don't tell Dad about it. Okay?"

They promised they would try not to.

"Where is he?" Jim asked.

"In the living room. And not feeling so great, either," Peg replied.

Jim took the drawing back upstairs to his room, then returned and entered the living room to talk with his father. Mr. Cort was sitting by the window, looking out at the street in apparent deep concentration.

"Hi, Dad," said Jim. "No luck finding a job?"

His father looked at him. "Hi, son. No, no luck. I didn't expect to find one right off the bat, anyway. I've filled out a couple applications, but if I don't hear from one of them within two months or so, I'm going to think seriously about looking for a job out of town. Don't worry. It'll be our last resort," he added quickly as Jim's face suddenly showed concern. "I know how you, Peg, and your mother feel about living here. I like it, too, but if I can't find work here we'll have to go where I can."

Jim nodded. "I understand, Dad."

"I've also applied for a course in advanced accounting," his father went on. "They're evening classes. They're running for eight weeks and are taught on Tuesdays and Thursdays. That, with the training I got in prison, should help me find a job fairly easily, I should think."

"I hope so, Dad," Jim said. "When does the course start?"

"It started last week. But I can start tomorrow night."

He tries to make it sound as if it will be simple to find a job with the course under his belt too, Jim thought. But he knew his father wasn't really sure he would. The stigma of serving time was going to remain with him until he found an employer who would say to him, "You're hired. Be here Monday morning at eight o'clock sharp."

The next two days of practice were spent mainly on defensive plays meant to cope with the strong offensive team the Rams were up against this coming Friday night, the Coral Town Indians. Coach Butler reminded his boys that the Indians had a running back who had been the second highest scorer last year and was heading for that title, or better, this year. His name was Roy Slate, and some of the reporters were already figuring he was big-time material. He liked to run. His tactic was to carry the ball around the ends, usually his left end. This meant, thought Jim, that Slate would be coming around his side of the line.

Coach Butler had Mark Taylor simulate Slate's anticipated moves, so when the fullback came tearing around Jim's side of the line, Jim tried to meet him with his shoulders down around Mark's knees. But Mark got excellent blocking from his linemen, and Jim found himself knocked back on his rear, while Mark raced by for what could have been a long run, or even a touchdown, in a game.

"You're not dodging the blockers, Jim!" Coach Butler yelled at him. "Use footwork! Isaacs, hit your man, and *then* go after the ballcarrier!" Ron Isaacs, a short, stocky kid who was faster than he looked, played right tackle.

On both Wednesday and Thursday nights Jim studied his notes and the play patterns that the coach said the Rams would be using against the Coral Town Indians. He was worried about his defensive playing. He knew he could stand a lot of improvement as a tackler, and was sure that Coach Butler was aware of that, too. He hoped he could help at least on one touchdown. Two or three would be better. But, from the number of plays he was involved in during the past several days, he wondered if he would see any action at all.

He studied the 14 right flat option thoroughly. In this play the quarterback took the pass from center, pedaled back behind the right halfback, then unleashed a long pass to either the fullback, or to the right end, who was running almost parallel with him. In this situation Jim was the right end.

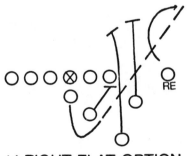

14 RIGHT FLAT OPTION

He stayed up till almost midnight Thursday, concentrating on the runs and pass plays. He had blocking assignments, too, but he felt that memorizing his offensive plays was more important than the defensive plays. Scoring came on the offensive plays.

Another play he hoped Chuck would call was the T 17 fly. This play called for a pass deep downfield. Jim and left end Dick Ronovitz scissor behind the line of scrimmage, while Chuck runs back after taking the ball from center, fakes a handoff to Mark, then heaves a pass to Jim.

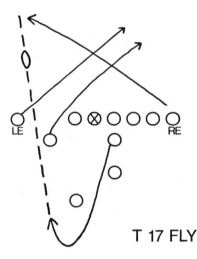

T 17 FLY

When he finally went to bed, his mind was a battleground of notes and football plays. But lurking in the background was an unseen face, in shadow, ready to make another malicious telephone call to him about his father.

He tossed and turned, throwing the covers off his hot, sweating body, then pulling them back on when he got cold. When he arose in the morning he didn't think he had slept at all. He thought he remembered seeing someone standing at the foot of his bed, someone he couldn't see clearly, except a pair of bright, staring eyes.

He guessed he must have looked as bad as he felt when he finally went downstairs and sat at the table for breakfast, because his mother stared at him as if he had suddenly contracted measles.

"What's the matter, son? Didn't you sleep last night?" she asked him.

"Not much, I guess," he admitted. "Where's Peg?"

"In the living room, cramming for an English test. And Dad's still in bed. He didn't sleep well, either."

Jim began to wolf down the scrambled eggs and toast his mother had made for him, and she tapped him on the shoulder.

"Slow down," she said. "You're not going to a fire."

He shook his head. "I guess I'm not all here," he said.

She poured herself a cup of coffee and sat on the chair beside him. "You're worked up over your father, aren't you?" she said quietly. "Between his coming home from prison, those phone calls and the drawing, and your trying to play football, you must feel pretty confused."

He nodded.

She poured a spoonful of sugar into the coffee, added milk, and stirred it. "First of all, son, remember this: officially your father paid for what he did. He served his term in prison, but he's going to keep on paying for it by just thinking about it, because he's that kind of a human being."

"I know, Mom," Jim said. "You don't have to tell me that."

"But I want to impress it on you," she replied firmly. "You don't know how sorry he is for what he's done, for what that foolish act has done to you and Peg, and me. You haven't seen the tears in his eyes like I have. You can't tell that his heart is broken."

"Mom —"

"Jim, what I'm trying to say is, don't let those phone calls or that drawing drive you crazy. Don't let any of the members of your football team interfere with your playing, or your school work. Get on the field and play as if none of those things have happened. I know it's difficult to do. But play as if you're playing for your father, as if he's the coach."

She paused, and Jim found that the heaviness that had lain in his stomach like a chunk of lead was almost gone.

He turned to his mother and smiled. "Did I ever tell you that you are one terrific mom?"

Her eyes glistened. "I don't need compliments.

But I'll accept them, gratefully." She leaned forward and kissed him.

Suddenly he remembered that his father had attended his first class the night before.

"How did Dad make out last night, Mom?" he asked.

Her eyes shone. "I guess all right. He said that the lessons were all a review to him." She winked. "I think he'll make out all right."

CHAPTER•8

IN SPITE of what his mother had told him, Jim found that trying to ignore the harassing phone calls and the drawing was impossible. He caught himself staring at the backs of several students in the classrooms throughout the morning, students who were members of the football team, wondering if one of them was guilty.

Twice a student turned and met his gaze squarely. The first time it was Steve Newton, the team's center. The second time it was Ben Culligan, the team's nose guard. Jim didn't know any reason why either of them might dislike him enough to torment him. They were good players. They were regulars. But if neither Pat Simmons nor Ed Terragano was the guilty one, maybe one of these good, regular players was.

Jim found Ben waiting for him in the corridor after class. A hundred-eighty-five-pound senior, Ben had led the team in tackles last year.

"Hey, man, what's with you?" he said to Jim,

his brown eyes snapping. "You on dope or something?"

Jim frowned. "Are you crazy? What are you talking about?"

"Why did you keep staring at me? Your eyes looked like one of those creeps you see in a monster movie."

"I'm sorry," said Jim. "I didn't mean to stare. I was just thinking, that's all."

"Well, think with your eyes stuck on someone else. Okay?" He glared at Jim and walked away, swaggering.

Count him innocent, Jim reflected, a smile crossing his lips.

He turned down the next corridor to head to his chemistry class when he heard the sharp click of heels approaching from behind him. Suddenly he felt a small, cool hand grab his wrist.

He turned. It was Margo.

"Hi," he said.

"Hi. What was that all about?"

His eyebrows arched. "What was what all about? Oh. With Ben? Nothing."

"Don't say nothing when I know it's something. I'm not blind, and I'm no dummy. I know something's been bothering you. I've noticed it ever since your father came home."

"Okay, Mother. You're right. But I don't want to talk about it," said Jim stiffly.

"Can we talk about it over lunch?"

"It doesn't concern you, Margo," Jim said seriously. "I don't want you to get mixed up in this."

He felt her fingers tighten on his wrist. "So it is something serious," she said. "Something more than your father coming home from prison."

He nodded. "It has something to do with that, yes," he admitted. "But — " He lowered his voice. "Margo," he said irritably, "this is my business. Okay? I'm going to handle it alone. My way."

She looked at him, unflinching. "I'd like to help you if I can, Jim."

His lips pursed. She was getting to be a pain.

He was ready to walk away from her when he suddenly thought of something.

"Wait a minute. You're in art class. Maybe you can help me." He was flushed with new hope all of a sudden.

Her eyes flashed. "Good!"

"I'll tell you about it at lunch."

A sparkle flickered in her eyes. "I can't wait!" she murmured excitedly.

He got to chemistry class and twice faced embarrassment when the teacher, Miss Lee, called on him to cite a couple of formulas that he didn't know. His penalty: to learn those two, plus two more he had to have for tomorrow.

His showing in math was no better. Miss Delray looked tired throughout class, but seemed fully awake when she ordered students to go up to the blackboard and write answers to problems. Jim feared he would be called, and he was. He wasn't able to complete the answer to the first problem he was asked to solve, and was saved by the bell on the second.

"I suppose if the problem pertained to a football situation — say the ball is on the enemy's ten-yard line, and it's third down — you wouldn't have any trouble at all working out the answer." Miss Delray's terse words drilled through the quiet classroom. "Or would you?"

"I'd run," Jim said.

The class roared.

"Class dismissed," Miss Delray ordered impassively.

Smiling, Jim went back to his desk, gathered up his books, and headed out of the room.

Barry caught up with him in the hall. "Jim, would you really have run?" he asked, frowning.

"Sure," said Jim. "For a pass."

He grinned, leaving Barry staring in puzzlement after him.

He took his books to his locker, went to the cafeteria, and found Margo waiting for him. They got in line, bought their lunch — macaroni and cheese, and milk — and went to sit at one of the tables.

"Okay, maestro, how can I help?" Margo asked before she even started to eat.

Jim downed a couple of forkfuls of macaroni

and cheese first, wondering if he was doing the right thing by getting her involved. Well, he had gone this far, he reflected. He might as well go all the way, particularly since she might be in a position to really help him.

"Did you know that I've been getting some crank phone calls?" he asked her.

Her eyes widened. "No. From whom?"

"That's the point. I don't know. From the sound of the voice I'm sure it's a male. But he muffles his voice so I can't identify it."

"So it's possible that you know him."

"Right."

She stabbed a few pieces of macaroni with her fork. "You don't have any idea who it is?"

"No. I thought it was Pat Simmons when I found a drawing stuck on our garage door and a drawing pencil with his name engraved on it near the pavement beside it. I think he felt like slugging me when I accused him of drawing the picture.

"What was the drawing?"

He explained it to her.

"Oh, for pete's sake," she exclaimed. "That is dirty. You think someone planted the pencil there to make you think Pat drew the picture?"

"That's what it looks like," said Jim. "Hey, you better start eating. You haven't even tasted your lunch yet."

"I've suddenly lost my appetite," she said. Nevertheless, she started to eat. "You still haven't told me how I could help," she said between bites.

"I'd like you to look at the drawing and tell me, if you can, who drew it. I showed it to Jerry when I thought it was Pat who had done it, but he said something about the lines being too strong, and the shading's different from Pat's work. Anyway, he was sure Pat didn't draw the picture. I thought maybe you might be able to tell."

"Where is it?"

"Home."

"Great. Now I'll be thinking all afternoon about whether or not I'll be able to figure out whose drawing it is. When can I see it?"

"Come over after school."

"Okay."

They ate for a while without talking. Jim soon had his plate cleaned, and finished drinking his milk.

"You know, Chick does a lot of extra drawing in class, I've noticed," Margo cut into the silence finally. "Would he have any reason to harass you?"

Jim picked up the napkin and wiped his mouth with it. "That's the point. I can't think of one lousy reason why anyone would want to harass me. But since my father's gotten out of prison, this person, whoever he is, has been driving me up a wall. It could be Chick. It could be anybody. But why, I don't know. I tell you, I can't sleep. When I do, I have nightmares. I'm unable to concentrate on my studies. I forget football plays. I'm going to be so tired tonight I might fall asleep on the field."

Margo placed her fork on her empty plate, wiped her mouth with her napkin, then leaned her elbows on the table. "One thing I gather from this," she said. "Someone wants you to quit the team."

Jim laughed. "You win a cigar."

"Someone who is pretending he's a friend of yours, but really and truly hates your guts."

Jim nodded. "That's the size of it."

The bell rang.

Margo looked at him. "Know what? I'm beginning to enjoy this. I've thought of being an airline pilot after I graduate from high school, but I think that being a detective could be a lot of fun, too!"

He frowned at her. "An airline pilot? You mean a stewardess, don't you?"

"A *pilot*. I know what I'm saying."

She came over to the house about four-thirty, took a look at the drawing, and her face paled.

"You think you know who drew it?" Jim asked, hope making his heart pound faster.

"I — I'm not sure. But some of it looks like Chick Benson's style. Those strong lines. The lips and the eyes. It's *definitely* his style."

"Then Chick's the guy!"

She raised her hand. "Maybe. Somebody else might have his style, too. It isn't that rare."

"Like who?"

"I don't know."

He took the drawing from her and refolded it. "My hunch is that you're on to something, Margo," he said. "Chick plays a roving backfield man on defense, but I think he'd like to play offense, too. Maybe Chick figures that he can worry me out of playing quicker than anybody else on the team."

"But you're still not sure, Jim," Margo argued seriously. "Making annoying phone calls and sticking a drawing on your garage that is supposed to symbolize your father's being an ex-con is quite a strong accusation to make against a guy who just wants to play offense on a football team."

Jim said sternly, "Nonetheless, it's a clue. It's something I can sink my teeth into."

She sighed. "What're you going to do? Show the drawing to Chick?"

"What do you think I should do?"

"Wait awhile. Try to find more proof that it's him."

He hesitated and finally agreed with her. "Okay. Maybe you're right."

He thanked her for her help, and she left. A thin smile fluttered across his lips. Chick, huh? he thought. I'll dig up more proof somewhere.

* * *

Jim was quiet as a dormouse at the dinner table. He had the eerie feeling that the phone would ring at any minute, that the same muffled voice was going to call him. Was it Chick?

At a quarter to six, just as he started to head upstairs to get ready to leave for the football field, the phone rang. Peg and his father seemed to freeze in their chairs in the living room. They watched him; he watched them.

Finally Peg got up. "I'll answer it," she said.

She got to the phone and said something into the receiver. Then, in a louder voice, she demanded, "Who is this? Who wants to speak to him?"

She held the receiver a moment longer, then lowered it to its cradle. Her hand was trembling.

"He hung up," she said.

Jim turned and continued up the stairs. Was that Chick? he thought bitterly. Could it be he who was trying to force him off the team, and drive him out of his mind in the process?

It was only because Jim wasn't going to let the caller feel that he was winning his dirty game that he got dressed and went to the football game. No matter what, he was going to keep on playing.

CHAPTER • 9

THE GAME got underway at eight o'clock under the lights. The stands were packed. The night was warm. Too warm, Jim thought. He was sweating even before the team went out on the field for their pregame warm-up exercises.

The Coral Town Indians won the toss and chose to receive. Mark's kick off the tee was an end-over-ender to the Indians' six-yard line. Their left halfback caught it and carried it back to their twenty-eight.

"Remember that Slate guy," Chick reminded Jim in the huddle. "Cover him like a tent."

Sure, I will, Chick, ol' boy, Jim thought, looking Chick straight in the eye. If Chick noticed any implication in the look, he didn't show it.

"If he gets by Jim, you take him, Randy," Chick said.

"Right."

"Let's go."

The Indians ran the ball for a two-yard gain through right tackle, then picked up four more on a rush through the line's other side.

Third and four.

"Okay, keep your eyes open," Chick said, looking at Jim.

The Indians changed from a T formation to a spread: the quarterback was behind the center, the left halfback and fullback spaced about five yards apart behind him, the right halfback about two yards behind and to the left of the left end. Roy Slate was the left halfback.

Nick Enders, the Indians' tall, wiry quarterback, called signals.

"Down!"

Jim, crouched at the line of scrimmage, kept his gaze straight ahead. But within his peripheral vision he could easily see the Indians' left halfback.

"Set!"

Jim dug his toes into the turf.

"Hut one! Hut —!"

Instinctively, Jim moved forward. A fraction of a second later both lines moved. A flag dropped. A whistle blew.

The players looked at the referee. The man in the striped shirt pointed at Jim, then spun his hands to indicate the infraction.

"Offside!" he yelled. "Number eighty-eight! Five yards!"

Jim couldn't believe it. Dumbfounded, he watched the ref pace off five yards from the line of scrimmage against the Rams, and spot the ball on the Indians' thirty-nine.

"First down!"

"Nice going, Cort," said a disgusted voice at Jim's elbow.

It was Pat.

Jim felt a pair of eyes probing him from the other side. "I said to watch Slate," Chick said indignantly, "not red dog him before the ball is snapped."

Jim said nothing. He had no excuse for doing what he had done.

The Indians tried two running plays, and gained a total of two yards. There was no doubt now in Jim's mind that their next play would be a pass. He prepared thoroughly for it, listening to the signals, waiting to move the instant he saw the opponents move.

In the back of his mind he remembered the off-side call on him. He had to be careful not to repeat that costly error.

"Hut one! Hut two!"

The Indians charged. Jim dodged the opposing end, lost his footing, then got up and sprang after Slate, who was sprinting down his left side of the field into Rams territory.

Jim bolted after him, closing the gap fast. It was

when Slate looked back and started to reach up and out that Jim, thinking that he was ready to pull down a pass, dove at the speeding back.

He got one hand on Slate's shirt and yanked. The garment ripped off Slate's back, the pull slowing him down just enough so that the ball sailed past his outreaching hands.

A flag dropped. Then another.

Jim stopped running, his eyes staring at the bouncing football.

"You crazy, man?" a soft voice grated at him. "I got to be near that ball first before you can tackle me."

Jim looked at Slate, met the tall athlete's eyes squarely, then looked away as he realized what he had done.

Chick picked up the ball and tossed it to the ref, who was standing in the exact spot where Jim had grabbed the intended receiver. Jim watched the official put the ball down on the turf, then listened to him announce the infraction.

"Number eighty-eight! Pass interference! First down!"

A voice barked, "Cort! Take off!"

Jim looked at Chick, then saw Barry Delaney come running in from the bench. Silent, he ran off the field. He saw an empty space on the bench and sat down.

The cheerleaders began to chant:

"CORT! C-O-R-T!
'RAAYYYYY!"

There was no reason to cheer him, Jim knew. He pulled off his helmet, caught a towel a kid tossed to him, and wiped his perspiring face.

Coach Butler came over and stood in front of him. His thick biceps stretched the short sleeves of his green shirt. The brim of his baseball cap, with the letters *PL* on it, was pulled down low, shading his piercing blue eyes.

"You don't tackle a receiver until he has the ball," Coach Butler said tersely.

"I know. I'm sorry," Jim said.

"Also, if you had looked back over your shoulder for just a second when you saw Slate reaching for the ball, you might have been able to make an interception," the coach went on. "Or knock the ball down, anyway."

Jim said nothing. But he had to admit that he had not thought of doing either of the things the coach mentioned.

The Indians kept surging and were stopped on the Rams' twenty-one. Their attempted field goal clicked for three points.

Indians 3, Rams 0.

Ed Terragano got to their own thirty-three-yard line on the kickoff. In four plays the Rams got the ball on the Indians' twenty-five. The Indians held them there for three downs, and Jim wondered if Chuck would call for a field-goal attempt or a punt. Mark was the Rams' kicker, but he had never attempted to kick more than a twenty-yard field goal before. With the ball on the twenty-five, the holder would take the snap about seven yards farther back, anyway, meaning that the kick would have to go more than forty-two yards to clear the uprights.

The Rams broke out of the huddle and went into punt formation. Chuck had made a wise call, Jim figured.

Mark tried to punt the ball out of bounds down near the five-yard line. It went out near the ten. Not bad, thought Jim.

But the Indians pulled off a long pass, and then a couple of good runs that got them deep into Rams territory again. Before the quarter was over they scored a touchdown.

Coach Butler sent Jim back in during the middle of the second quarter. The ball was the Rams' on the Indians' forty-two-yard line.

Mark plowed through right tackle for a four-yard gain, then was stopped dead on the scrimmage line on another line-plunging attempt.

In the huddle, Chuck looked from one face to another as if waiting for someone to offer a suggestion.

"We've got to get on the scoreboard, you guys,"

he said finally. "How about the scissor pass?"

The pass play struck a chord in Jim's memory. It called for him to run ahead five yards, then swing to the left. Dick Ronovitz would run it the same way, only in the opposite direction.

For a few seconds no one reacted to the suggestion. Jim felt a nervous twitch on the side of his jaw, thinking that the guys weren't in favor of seeing him in the act.

Suddenly Chuck clapped his hands. "We'll try it," he said. "On three."

They broke out of the huddle. The team lined up in position and Chuck began barking signals. On the three count, Steve snapped the ball. Chuck took it, faded back, and faked a handoff to Ed. Ed started an end-around run, then got into a pocket formed by Steve and the tackles. Jim cut across the field and saw Dick running past him.

An Indian guard chased after Jim, but Jim figured there were at least five yards between them, a gap he was sure he could maintain. He was near the Indians' ten-yard line when he decided to glance back for Chuck's pass. By now the gap between him and his guard had increased by at least another yard.

But Chuck wasn't passing to him. He was passing to Dick down the right flat instead!

Dick's guard was within arm's reach of him; nothing but a perfect throw would work. A couple feet short and the pass could be intercepted. A couple feet too far ahead of Dick and he wouldn't be able to catch it.

The pass was perfect. Dick caught it on his fingertips, pulled it against his chest, and kept out of reach of his pursuer long enough to cross the goal line.

Jim watched the guys run to Dick, slap him on the back, thump him on the rump.

Anger ignited in Jim and flared for a while, but he tried to control it. It was clear as day that he had been the better choice for Chuck to throw to than Dick, yet Chuck had neglected him.

Jim shook his head. What was happening? Why couldn't he feel good that his team had scored? Why was he so uptight?

In front of the Rams fans, the cheerleaders leaped, somersaulted, then led in a cheer:

"R-O-N-O-V-I-T-Z!
Ronovitz! 'Raaayyyyy!"

The teams lined up, and Mark kicked for the point after. It was good. Indians 10, Rams 7.

Jim fought an impulse to complain to Chuck about the play. Why shouldn't he say something about it? Why not clear the air with Chuck, get an explanation from him about why he had thrown to Dick instead of to Jim?

No, he decided. Heck, why make things worse? Jim knew why he was being ignored.

Unfair! How many of you have saints for fathers? he felt like yelling at them.

The Indians had possession of the ball on the Rams' eighteen when the two-minute-warning whistle blew.

"You can bet your boots Enders will try at least a couple of passes to score again before the half's over," Chick said in the huddle. "Cover Slate. Cover him good."

"We don't want to forget their other end," reminded Fred Yates. "He caught a few short passes, too."

"Let's blitz 'em," suggested Ben Culligan. "That'll force him to throw. Maybe before he can find a target."

"I'll buy that," said Steve Newton, playing linebacker on defense.

"Okay. I'll buy that, too," Chick agreed. "But watch Slate like a hawk. I mean you two guys, Cort and Dick."

Cort and Dick. Did Chick use Jim's last name and Dick's first because they were shorter? Or was it because "Cort" was more formal, and the use of it meant that Chick and Jim were not on the same friendly basis anymore that they once had been?

Jim found himself thinking all sorts of crazy thoughts. I've got to stop this, he told himself.

The whistle blew, signaling the end of the two minutes. The teams lined up at the line of scrimmage.

"Set!" barked Enders, the Indians' quarterback. "Eighteen!"

The lines braced. Enders scanned the defense. "Blue!"

Was this the audible or not? Jim thought. You never know, and you can't guess. The offense can change it anytime they wished. You just had to wait and see.

"Forty-eight!"

Jim tensed. Was this a new play? Had the Rams formed a defense that forced the Indians to change their play?

"Hut one! Hut two!"

The ball was snapped. Enders took it, faked a pass to his left halfback, turned, and handed the ball to his fullback. Out in the right flat Jim headed toward Roy Slate, the Indians' wide receiver. But the play was back there near the line, where the Indians' fullback had been blitzed and had fumbled the ball. Scott McDonald, the Rams left tackle, recovered it on their own sixteen.

"Hate to say it, but I will," Ben Culligan remarked as he started to head off the field to let the offense take over. "The blitz worked, didn't it?"

"Can't guess 'em wrong all the time, Cully!" Pat Simmons replied.

The offense came in quickly — the few who didn't play both ways — got in a huddle, and Chuck immediately called for the scissor pass.

"Coach Butler's idea," he added.

Jim looked at him through narrowed eyes. How would the play work this time?

"Look," said Jim indignantly, "you sound as if you don't like to see me in any play. Maybe I might as well not be. You'll probably throw it to Dick, anyway."

Chuck met his eyes. "You haven't been catching the ball, Jim," he said grimly. "Maybe you haven't washed the grease off your hands. And you've been messing up the plays, tackling a receiver before he gets the ball, jumping the gun before the ball is snapped." His eyes glittered. "I just don't want to take chances, that's all. All right? I want to win this game. Bad."

A whistle blew. The players looked up.

"Delay of game!" yelled the ref. "Five-yard penalty!"

"Oh, great," Chuck grunted disgustedly. "Nothing like giving them the ball game. Come on. Let's get with it. The scissor."

They got to the line of scrimmage, which was now at the eleven-yard line instead of the sixteen. Chuck called signals, faked a handoff to Mark, then faded back to pass. Neither receiver was in the clear. Just as he was about to be tackled,

Chuck heaved the ball toward Jim, but so far over his head that it landed out of bounds.

Second and fifteen.

"How much time?" Chuck asked a ref.

"Fifty-three seconds," replied the official.

"Let's try it again," said Chuck in the huddle.

They tried the scissor again, and again Chuck heaved the ball to Jim. But an Indian defenseman sprang out of nowhere, leaped, and caught the pass. There was only one defensive man in his way between him and the goal, Pat Simmons. Pat hit him low, getting him on the twenty-one-yard line.

"Time!" yelled Chuck, and asked the ref again how much time was left.

"Forty-four seconds," said the ref.

"How many more time-outs do we have?" Pat wanted to know.

"This is it, fella," the ref replied.

The Rams' defense came running out. Among them was Barry Delaney.

"Take off, Jim," he said, jerking up a thumb.

CHAPTER • 10

JIM WATCHED the rest of the first half from the bench. He had not heard who was supposed to be responsible for that interception, but whose fault could it be if it weren't Chuck DeVal's? Chuck had just thrown the ball too short of his target, that was all.

With the ball on their own twenty-one, the Indians tried a line plunge and were held. Then, with only a few seconds left to play, they tried a field goal. It was good.

Two seconds later the first half was over. The Indians led, 13–7.

The Rams headed for the locker room and the inevitable talk by Coach Butler. All went except Jim. He remained on the bench, his helmet on the ground in front of him, his elbows on his knees, his hair blowing in the wind.

Why should I go? he asked himself. He wasn't wanted, anyway. Chuck said he was messing up the plays, and Chuck was right.

But why didn't that wise-guy quarterback realize why he, Jim, was messing up the plays? Even though Chuck didn't know about the harassing phone calls and the drawing, he should be able to tell that something was bothering Jim. If Chuck did sense something wrong, perhaps he didn't care.

Jim heard feet pounding and saw a shadow sweep up in front of him and stop.

"Jim! Are you all right?"

He looked up at Margo. "Yeah, I'm all right." He grabbed his helmet and rose to his feet. "Half the guys treat me like dirt, the other half ignore me. I might as well take my shower and go home."

"Most of that could be in your head, Jim," she said. "You're so bothered about those phone calls and that drawing that you think everyone is against you. That isn't true. Maybe there are a few who have a grudge, but not all of them."

"Oh, what do you know?" he said irritably, and started to head toward the school.

She touched his arm. "Jim."

He stopped and looked at her.

"Don't give up," she urged. "Don't quit. Your dad and your sister are in the stands. They came to see you play."

"Yeah, I know," he said.

He turned from her and continued on his way, her words about his father and sister ringing in his mind. He felt an ache in his throat and suddenly felt glad that he was alone.

Before he entered the school he wiped his eyes with his knuckles. He had always loved football; but, at that moment, he hated it.

The Indians kicked off to start the second half. Ed Terragano caught the end-over-end kick and carried it back to the Rams' twenty-two.

They gained eight yards on two right tackle runs. Then Chuck hit Ed on a long forward pass that put them on the Indians' thirty-one.

"We're rolling," Chuck said, sweat glistening on his proud face. "Another run, Mark?"

"How about a reverse for a change?" Pat cut in.

"Using the ends, you mean?" Chuck asked, glancing at him.

"No. Using Ed and Tony."

Jim felt his face redden. He shot a quick glance at Chuck, then lowered his gaze.

"Okay. I'll fake to Mark and hand off to Tony."

"What about an audible?"

"We won't need to call a color," said Chuck. "On three. Let's go."

They broke out of the huddle, and Chuck started calling signals. On the third "Hike!" Steve centered the ball. Chuck took it, faked a handoff to Mark — who went through the line as if he were carrying the ball — then handed the ball to

Tony. Tony sprinted behind the line toward the left side of the field, then handed the ball to Ed as the left halfback came sprinting toward the right side of the field.

Jim blocked his man, fell to his knees, sprang to his feet again to follow up on a block against another oncoming Coral Town Indian. The man got by him. Jim made a last-ditch attempt to stop him and barely touched the player's right ankle, but it was enough to make the man lose his balance and fall.

"*Shreeek!*" went a whistle. The play stopped.

Jim, still on the turf, glanced around to see what the call was.

"Clipping!" said the ref, striking the back of his right calf to indicate the infraction. "Number eighty-eight! Fifteen yards!"

Jim groaned, and took his time getting to his feet.

"You're really making a mess of this game, Cort," Pat snapped at him. "Why don't you pretend you got a twisted ankle or something?"

A player came running out. It was Barry.

"Out, Jim," he said.

Jim took a deep breath and let it out, then ran off the field. He sat down, expecting either Coach Butler or Coach Gibson to approach and remind him that clipping was one of the most foolish kinds of penalties; you just don't block a guy from behind him.

But neither coach came by, and Jim was thankful he had a few minutes to try to gather his wits together.

The game went on, and he watched the Rams keep the Indians from gaining a first down, thus forcing the opponents to kick. Once again the ball was in the Rams' possession, and in three plays Chuck got the boys to threaten the Indians again. His long pass to Ed netted fifty-four yards, getting the ball down on the Indians' fourteen-yard line.

Chuck tried two more passes in succession, but only gained a yard on the first and two on the second.

Third and seven to go.

"Jim, go in there," Coach Butler ordered. "Tell Chuck to use the forty-nine fly. Send Barry out. Hurry."

"Yes, sir."

Jim sprang off the bench, fastening his helmet as he bolted out on the field. He pointed at Barry, jerked a thumb, and Barry sprinted off the field, not looking very pleased about the change.

The team huddled. "Forty-nine fly," Jim relayed the coach's instructions.

He felt ten pairs of eyes look at him as he relayed the message.

"Okay," Chuck said. "Forty-nine fly it is. On your toes, Ed."

The play called for Jim to dash straight up the field, then out to the right flat, and for Ed to do the same, except in the opposite direction. The pass was to go to Ed.

The team broke out of the huddle and went to the line of scrimmage. Chuck barked signals. The ball was snapped. The men blocked, the halfs faked. The pass was thrown deep into the left flat, and Ed pulled it in just over the end zone.

The whole play went off exactly as planned.

Mark kicked for the point after, but the ball missed the uprights by inches. A sick groan came from the Rams' fans and died away almost as quickly as it started.

Indians 13, Rams 13.

In the fourth quarter, the Indians got the ball down to the Rams' twenty-eight and twice tried to rush for another first down and failed.

Two minutes before the end of the game they were on the twenty-three with five yards to go. It was third down.

They passed. Jim watched the ball and sprinted for a possible interception. He leaped for the ball just as it headed down toward the intended receiver's hands, grabbed it — then dropped it.

"Bull!" he said, disgusted.

The Indians went on for a three-pointer and made it. They copped the game, 16–13.

They and their fans whooped it up for a while on the field; a prelude, Jim thought, to the celebration they would have when they returned home.

He headed off the field alone, feeling partly responsible for the loss. He had played a lousy game, and he'd be the first to admit it.

"Jim!"

He recognized the soft, warm voice and stopped. Margo approached, wearing her white sweater now with the large letters, *PL*, on the front of it.

"Yeah?"

"I just want to say you did all right," she said.

"I did lousy."

He turned away from her and continued on toward the exit. She grabbed his arm. "I learned something about a couple of the guys. Not much, but something."

He stopped again and looked at her. "About whom?"

"Chick and Steve."

He frowned and pursed his lips. People were sweeping past them in droves: men, women, and kids.

"This is no place to talk about it," he said.

"How about tomorrow?" she suggested. "At Freddie's, over a Coke or something."

"Okay. Meet you there at two o'clock."

She smiled, spun on her toes, and stitched her way quickly through the throng. What had she learned about Chick and Steve? he wondered. It was going to be a long time until two o'clock tomorrow.

He went on to the locker room, undressed,

showered, and met Peg at the exit door. They walked to the parking lot where their parents were waiting in the car for them. They got in.

"Good game," his father said as he started the car.

"Don't be so kind, Dad," Jim replied. He was sitting in back with Peg, feeling clean and fresh from the shower. If he could only cleanse away the problem that plagued him as easily as he could the sweat and dirt, he thought dismally.

"What do you think I'd say?" his father asked, backing the car out of the space, then shooting it toward the street. "That you played a terrible game? Under the circumstances you did well. Real well."

"You showed you had guts," his mother added firmly. "In my book that comes before anything else."

Jim smiled. "Thanks, Mom."

"Now that, dear brother," Peg chimed in, "comes from a real pro. Right, Mother?"

"Right!"

CHAPTER•11

JIM AND MARGO sat in a corner booth of Freddie's Diner, each sipping Coke through long yellow straws. A recent country hit was blaring from the lavishly painted jukebox set in another corner of the restaurant.

"Okay," said Jim. "Chick was picked up for smoking pot when he was ten years old. What's that got to do with those phone calls and the drawing?"

"Don't you see? He might be a guy who goes out of his way to get into trouble. Chick is no angel. Believe me. I know."

Jim's eyes narrowed suspiciously. For a moment he ignored the main reason of their meeting here. "How do you know?"

"I'm a woman, that's how. And a woman instinctively knows certain things about certain kinds of men."

"Is that so?"

"Yes, that's so!" she declared.

Her voice must have carried to the table across from them, because the patrons sitting there suddenly turned with interest to look at her.

"Keep it down," said Jim, slightly embarrassed. He cleared his throat. "What did you do? Go out with him?"

"Do I have to go out with him to learn certain things about him? No, I didn't go out with him. What I've learned about him is just from things he said, and things other girls have told me." Her eyes widened. "Don't you think that's plenty of evidence?"

"Margo, nothing you've said proves he is the one who's been bothering me."

She glared at him. "Yesterday you were ready to hang him. Now you sound like one of those defense lawyers on TV."

"I've taken the time to think about things," he told her.

Not taking her eyes off him, she put her mouth around the straw and took a long drag on her Coke.

"What did you learn about Newton?" Jim asked.

She took the straw out of her mouth. Her tone was softer now as she answered him. "Steve Newton was in art class but dropped out because he couldn't carry five subjects. He was a good artist and would have preferred to stay in it, but art carried only half a point against a whole point for the other subjects."

"Well, that proves he can draw," Jim said. "What else has he done that makes you think he can be a suspect?"

Margo laid her elbows on the table top, leaned forward, and whispered, "Did you know that about a year ago he was caught making harassment calls to people over the telephone?"

Jim, leaning forward to hear what she said, shook his head. "No. Who told you?"

She shrugged and smiled. "My source. And you know what newspaper reporters say about their sources. They won't tell on them."

Jim wanted to remind her that she wasn't a newspaper reporter, but, instead, said that he didn't think that Steve would be dumb enough to pull a sick thing like that again after he'd been caught.

Somehow he was disappointed. He thought that she might have discovered something more concrete.

"That's it?" he asked.

"That's it," she echoed. She cupped her chin in her hands. "You don't think that's enough evidence to check them out any further?"

He shrugged his shoulders. "To tell the truth, I don't know," he said. "But I doubt it. Anyway, don't give up. We still shouldn't let any stone go unturned."

She smiled graciously. "I guess that's my point," she said.

He finished his Coke, down to the last drop. "Know what? I think we'd make a pretty good detective team."

Her eyebrows arched. "Hey! What a terrific idea!"

He thought about it a moment, and sighed. "Forget it," he said, pushing his chair back with a grating noise. "The best ones are always married."

The day went by, and so did Monday and Tuesday without a phone call from the mystery caller. Jim began to have hopes that the person had gotten tired of his lousy joke and stopped it.

But, on Wednesday, there was a letter in the mailbox addressed to him. The address was made up of letters cut out of a magazine.

The hard lump that had begun to leave his stomach was suddenly back again. The jokester was using a different tack to get at him.

But it was something more than just a letter he had written, Jim observed. The envelope was too thick for just a single piece of stationery.

Jim started to head to his room with it. He preferred not to open it in the presence of his parents and Peg, feeling that whatever was in it would only stir them up again.

"Jim?" His mother's voice stopped him. "Aren't you going to open up that letter?"

He looked around at her. They were in the kitchen: she, Peg, and he. His father was in the living room, probably studying his accounting lesson.

"If you don't mind, Mom, I'd rather open it up in my room," he said.

"It's from that character, isn't it?"

She had brought the letter in from the mailbox. She had seen the address on it.

"I think so," Jim said.

Peg gazed contemplatively at him, her white teeth biting down gently on a side of her bottom lip. "I think you should let us know what's in that letter, Jim," she said. "What's been happening to you has been affecting us, too, you know."

"I know, Peg," Jim agreed. "But I think I can handle it. And I'm not doing it alone."

"Oh? Who's helping you?"

"Margo. Margo Anderson. She's in some of the classes that most of the football players are in, and is doing some checking for me. If you tried to do it, you might not get anywhere."

"Because I'm your sister, you mean?"

"Right." He turned and headed for the stairs. "I'll be down for dinner."

In his room he read the address again. Then, his hands shaking, he tore open the envelope with his forefinger and drew out a folded picture and a sheet of plain white paper on which were two words: YOU SMELL! They were cut out separately from what appeared to be a page of a magazine.

Jim unfolded the picture, which had also been cut out of a magazine. It was of a thief wearing a mask and carrying a gun. He was stepping out of a room through a window with a bag in one hand.

Jim pressed his lips firmly together to suppress his anger. His fingers tightened on the picture. He was about to crush it and crumble it into a tiny ball, when a thought occurred to him. If the picture was taken from a magazine, which it apparently was because the paper was slick, then the magazine's name might be printed somewhere on it. How its name might help him, Jim had no idea. But he could use every clue he could find.

He met with disappointment. Neither the name of the magazine nor the date was on the page. Only the page numbers, 55 and 56, were on it. He turned the page over and found that the name and date were not on that side, either.

Great. His chance of trying to figure out what magazine the page came out of was next to zero.

Wait a minute. There were two two-column advertisements on the page. Both of them said something about stocks. Was it a clue? Maybe.

He began to read the printed column that started off with: "(*continued from page 52*): *investments pay lower yields than taxable investments.*

But you can adjust for the tax bite and end up with more money to keep, tax-free, than with income you have to pay tax on."

There was more, and all on the same topic: investments.

Jim narrowed his eyes. There was hardly any doubt about it. The page was cut out of a magazine that dealt with investments. Or, in a general sense, stocks.

Did the mystery caller buy the magazine from a newsstand? Or was he, or a member of his family, a subscriber?

It was a clue. A thin one, but a clue.

Jim saw a glimmer of hope shining on the horizon as he refolded the picture, stuck it into his shirt pocket with the YOU SMELL! message, and went back downstairs. He preferred not to mention the items to the rest of his family who were already congregating around the dining room table for dinner, but conscience, and the expression in his mother's and Peg's eyes, got the best of him.

He showed all three the message and the picture. His mother's reaction upon reading them was consternation and anger. So was Peg's. And Jim was not surprised.

What surprised him was the look on his father's face when he saw the items. There was despair and pain in it, not anger, not hate.

Handing the items back to Jim, he said compassionately, "It's a sick person who's doing that to you, Jim. Try not to get upset about it. The problem is his, not yours."

"Maybe it is, Dad," agreed Jim, stuffing the folded pages back into his shirt pocket. "But I intend to find out who's doing it. Sick or not, he's driving me up a wall."

"You don't have a single idea who it is?" Peg asked, placing a steaming hot dish of bean casserole on the table.

"Not exactly. But it's somebody on our football team. It's got to be."

She focused her attention on him. "I hope you don't suspect Chuck."

"You're right. I don't. But have you noticed how many plays I've been involved in in the last two games?"

"I know. Not many," she said. "But maybe that's because you —" She paused, and looked away from him. "I'm sorry. Let's drop it."

"Fine by me," said Jim.

His father and mother, he noticed, gave each other a long, speculative look. They said nothing, though, as if they, too, didn't care to pursue the subject any further.

After dinner, Jim telephoned Margo and asked her if she could meet him in fifteen minutes at the public library.

"Sure," she answered. "But why the library?"

" 'Cause it's nice and quiet there," he told her.

CHAPTER • 12

IT WAS five after seven and already growing dark. The Port Lee Public Library, on Chickamaw Street, had all its lights turned on.

Jim and Margo sat alone at a large mahogany table near the rack holding a variety of magazines. Jim had shown her the contents of the envelope he had received, had put the sheet with YOU SMELL! on it back into his pocket, and left the other, with the stock advertisements face up, in front of him.

"What I think we ought to do," he said as quietly as he could and still be sure she heard him, "is find out which magazine this page was cut out of."

"And then?"

"Find out who subscribes to it."

Margo's eyebrows arched. "You make it sound so simple."

"Okay. You got a better idea?"

"No."

"Okay. Let's grab up the magazines dealing with stocks and bonds and check them to see which one has the same size page as this."

They got up, approached the magazine rack, and selected three magazines dealing with stocks and bonds. All three resembled each other in size, but only one of them had the pages the exact size as the one showing the picture of the thief. It was *Stocks in Review.*

"One down, three to go," said Jim, tingling with his success.

Margo looked at him. "How do you figure?"

"On the next down we find out which issue the picture was cut out of," Jim replied, the order of progress clear in his head. "On the third down we find out whom we know who subscribes to it."

"And on the fourth?"

"We score a touchdown."

Margo laughed. "Okay, quarterback! You've got the ball!"

Jim saw that the magazine he was holding was the September issue. He flipped its pages and found, to his disappointment, that the page, 55–56, was not the same as the one mailed to him.

"Bull," he said, and returned the three magazines to the rack. He looked at the others carefully, and a glimmer of hope fanned in him as he saw that there was at least one more copy of each magazine. The August issue of *Stocks in Review* was one of them.

He removed it, flipped its pages, and came to 55–56. It was the same page as the one mailed to him!

"Margo!" he exclaimed. "I've found it! It came out of the August issue!"

"Fine! Now what?"

"Now comes the hard part," he said, his voice becoming softer. "You have to make some phone calls."

"Oh, I do, do I? To whom?"

"The suspects."

She frowned and pushed back her chair. "You mean Chick and Steve?"

"Chick, Steve, and even Chuck," said Jim. "Let's go. Tell them you're Ms. So-an'-so and want to know if they would like to subscribe to *Stocks in Review* magazine."

He picked up a short yellow pencil and a sheet of paper from the top of an index file, then he and Margo went outside. A phone booth was just past the exit door. He found the phone numbers of the Bensons, the Newtons, and the DeVals in the directory and wrote them down.

Margo dialed the Benson number first. Her suddenly nervous-looking eyes told Jim that someone was answering her ring.

"Hello? Mrs. Benson?" Margo said sweetly.

"How do you do? I'm Ms. Bailey. Are you, or your husband, already subscribers to *Stocks in Review* magazine?"

There was a moment of silence as Jim watched Margo listening to the reply.

Then Margo, cracking a faint smile, said, "Thank you, Mrs. Benson. Have a nice day."

She hung up and stared at Jim. "Mr. Benson's already a subscriber!"

"Hey! Good!" Jim wrote yes after the Benson name. "Now try the Newtons."

She dialed again, got an answer, and apparently an abrupt reply, because she placed the receiver back on the cradle fast and looked at Jim with soft, hurt eyes. "Wow! Was she snippy!"

"Subscriber or not?"

"Not."

Jim wrote no after the Newton name. "DeVal next," he said.

Margo dialed the DeVals' number and almost immediately started her spiel. When she hung up, Jim felt sure they had scored again.

But Margo said, "Mr. DeVal gets the magazine now and then from a friend. She, Mrs. DeVal, is quite sure he wouldn't care to subscribe to it."

"Can't blame him," said Jim. He sighed. "Well, one out of three." He held up a finger. "We've got to get that August issue from the Bensons and see if page fifty-five and fifty-six is intact or ripped out."

"How do you expect to accomplish that?"

He grinned mischievously, grabbed her small chin, and gently squeezed it. "You did so well telephoning, you should do well with that assignment, too, Detective Anderson."

"Aren't you sweet," she said impishly.

He took his wallet out of his pocket, counted the money in it, and put it back. "Just enough for a couple of root beer floats," he said. "What do you say?"

She grabbed his arm. "I say sure!" She beamed delightedly.

With long, happy strides they walked out of the library into the lighted street.

"Jim," Margo said as they headed down the sidewalk toward the Burger Queen two blocks away, "if Chick's the guilty party, what are you going to say to him?"

"I don't know," replied Jim. "But I'll figure out something. When are you going to see Mrs. Benson about that August issue?"

"Tomorrow. Maybe tomorrow night. I don't know."

"The sooner the better," said Jim.

He felt cool, calm, and collected. They were making progress. It wouldn't be much longer before they would know who had made those malicious phone calls, drawn the obscene picture, and mailed him the picture torn out of a *Stocks in Review* magazine.

Football practice went on as usual on Thursday afternoon, except for one thing: Jim wasn't able to function without thinking that Chick Benson might be the culprit who was trying to undermine his playing ability. Jim forgot defensive plays. Twice he blocked the wrong man. Once he grabbed a guy's face guard. Another time he threw a block on a guard, then saw the ballcarrier sweep around him for a clean twenty-yard run before Chick and Pat Simmons nailed him.

"Where have you got your head, Cort?" Pat snapped at him. "You haven't done a thing right yet."

Jim said nothing. He had an excuse, but it wouldn't be accepted. Not here. Not yet.

"Jim!" a deep voice shouted from the sideline. "Come here!"

Jim yanked off his helmet and trotted off the field. Coach Butler stood in front of the bench, players standing on both sides of him. Perched on top of the bench almost directly behind him was Jerry Watkins, his ever-present camera hung from a strap around his neck. Jim saw he had the camera focused on him.

Waste an exposure, Jerry, Jim wanted to tell him. Waste a couple. What have you got? A scrapbook of failures, too?

He came up alongside the coach.

"Jim, I can't believe you're doing all those crazy

things out there," Coach Butler declared. "You're playing like a kid just starting small-fry football."

Jim looked for a towel on the bench, saw one, picked it up and wiped his face.

"I'm sorry, Coach. But I'll get over it. I promise."

"I can't depend on promises," the coach retorted. He spat and yanked on his baseball cap. His other hand was deep inside the breast pocket of his blue nylon jacket. "Grabbing the face mask was just plain dumbness. But letting a flanker sweep by you and you don't even know he's going — for pete's sake, man, that could mean seven points in a game. Know what I'm saying?

"Have you forgotten the block and attack?" he went on. "Hit your guard, yes, but then rush on after that guy with the ball if he comes around your end. And what have you been doing on the second down and seven- or eight-to-go plays? Or on the third down and six-to-go plays? You're rushing hard, but you're not dropping back for the pass. You're playing according to your own logic, Jim, not signal. Know what I'm saying?"

"Yes."

"Yes," he echoed, mockingly. "Don't just say yes to say yes. Are you sure?"

Jim nodded. "I'm sure."

The coach stared at him. Then his voice lowered. "Your Dad get a job yet?"

"Not yet."

"He will. He's a good guy. And he's doing fine in that accounting course."

Jim stared at him. "How —"

"One of our teachers is teaching it," the coach cut in. "Okay. Get out there. And keep your mind on the game. All right?"

Jim nodded. He put his helmet back on and ran out on the field, much faster than he had run off.

The coach was a real man, he thought. Through and through he was fourteen carat.

Jim tried to get himself together, and on signal he charged forward on the pass plays, then rushed back to cover his man in case he was the intended receiver. Once — and once was a lot right now — he pulled down an interception.

"Nice going, Jim," said Chick.

A compliment from Chick? Jim was confused. Would a guy who wanted him off the team compliment him on a play? Did he do it to throw Jim off his track if he suspected that Jim was trying to find out who the culprit was?

Jim had no way of knowing — yet.

He grabbed two receptions after a run of some twenty yards, one of which he had to leap up for in front of Chick Benson. Chick went down and rolled over before coming back up on his feet, unhurt. That he felt disgusted with himself for failing to intercept the pass was clear on his face.

Jim's smile came and vanished as quickly. He'd save it for a later time.

The tiger roll, then five laps around the field, completed the practice session. On their way to the school and the showers, Jim found himself walking beside Pat. He remained quiet, not caring to be intimidated by Pat, but it was Pat who broke the silence between them.

"Hey, you find out who drew that picture?"

Jim looked at him, surprised that he should mention it. "Not yet."

"You trying?"

"Yup."

"No idea who did it?"

"Not yet." Jim frowned. "You wouldn't have any suggestions, would you?"

"Me? Heck, no."

Jim hesitated. "Would you tell me if you did?"

Their eyes met. A faint smile came over Pat's mouth. "Yes, I would. You know, I've been thinking. I carried a grudge against you, and your father, earlier. I couldn't help it. But I heard what your father's doing and I think it's great. And I know you're having it tough, with the team and all."

Jim smiled back. "Thanks, Pat. You're okay."

"It's very easy to be a jerk," Pat said. "Guess that's what I was."

They entered the locker room, stripped, and took their showers.

CHAPTER • 13

JIM WAS in his father's den, typing up some of the play patterns the team would be using during tomorrow night's game against the Floralview Bucs. The door was open and he heard the front bell ring.

He paused, wondering who it was. Then he heard the door close, and the muffled sound of footsteps on the rug. The footsteps seemed to be approaching the den.

He looked toward the door and saw Peg. She had her hand raised, ready to knock on the door casing.

"Hi, brother," she said. "Someone to see you."

Then he saw Margo.

"Hi, Margo. Come in."

"Thank you."

Peg smiled and left, and Margo entered the den. She had her hair tied in a ponytail, and her hands stuck inside the pockets of her maroon imitation-leather jacket.

"Want to sit?" Jim invited.

"Thanks."

She chose the black leather lounging chair his father had often used when he took his nap, the days when he had a steady job and came home hungry and bone tired. Since his release from prison, he hadn't sat or slept on the chair more than half a dozen times.

"I hope I'm not too late," she said. She reached back and pulled her hair out from behind her jacket collar.

Jim looked at the electric clock on top of his father's desk. It was twenty after seven.

"It's early," he said. "What do you think we do, go to bed with the chickens?"

She laughed. "Hey, what a lovely room," she exclaimed, looking at the wall plaques, the pictures of birds and animals, and the wood carvings of pelicans on a shelf. "Yours?"

"My father's. This is his room. Well, did you get the magazine from the Bensons?"

She turned to him. "I had a girl friend get it for me," she answered. "But it was all intact."

He frowned, disappointed.

"I'm afraid we were barking up the wrong tree," she said.

"Bull!" Jim shook his head. "We're back to square one!"

"Jim, how about Barry?"

He stared at her. "Barry Delaney? You crazy? He's a good friend of mine. He wouldn't do things like that."

"He's not a regular player on the team," she said. "And I've noticed the look on his face at times when he goes in to take your place, and at times when you go in to replace him. Going in, he looks proud as a peacock. Coming out, he looks sad and hurt. Mostly hurt."

"Margo! It's not Barry! I know it isn't!"

She shrugged and threw out her hands. "Then you're right. We're back to square one. With a high fence all around it."

Barry? Jim shook his head. Barry was a softie, a pussycat. He wouldn't — he couldn't — do a dirty thing like making those phone calls.

"What are you thinking?" Margo broke into his thoughts. "You've got your face screwed up like a dried-up prune."

"I'm thinking about Barry," he said. "And what you said about how happy he looks when he plays, and how disgusted he looks when he doesn't. Maybe you're right. Maybe he's jealous of me and is using my father's release from prison to get at me."

"Is his father a stocks-and-bonds man?" Margo asked.

"I don't know. But I'm going to find out." He paused and indulged in more thinking. Suddenly his face lit up. "I know what. I'll have my mother call his mother tomorrow while we're in school, and ask her if Mr. Delaney subscribes to *Stocks in Review.* If he does, maybe she can borrow the August issue for me."

"I hate to say this, but it would be terrible if he's the guy," said Margo. "He's your neighbor."

"Telling me? We've been friends ever since they moved next door." Jim bit on his lower lip until it hurt. "Darn! I hate to think of him pulling those lousy things on me, Margo!"

She shrugged and stood up.

"I've got to go. See you tomorrow," she said.

A few minutes later Jim stepped out of the room and called to his mother. "Mom! Can I see you a minute, please?"

"All right!" came her reply from the living room.

He stepped back into the room and waited for her. She soon came, leaned against the doorframe, and crossed her hands in front of her.

"Hi, Mom." He cleared his throat. "I've got a favor to ask of you."

"Just keep it simple," she said.

Calmly, he told her what he would like her to do. When he was finished, she looked at him thoughtfully. "You suspect Barry?"

He shrugged. "At this point I don't know whom to suspect anymore, Mom. But Margo and I think it's possible that he's the guy. Anyway, we'd like to check him out."

"I think you're wrong," his mother said. "But I'll see what Frieda says."

"Thanks, Mom."

The next day during lunchtime Jim called his mother from a pay phone in the school cafeteria.

"You may have hit the jackpot," she told him.

His heart jumped. "Mr. Delaney subscribes to the magazine?"

"No. But he gets it from someone else "

"From whom?"

"Mr. Watkins. Mr. G. T. Watkins."

G. T. Watkins? Jim's hand tightened on the receiver. "Did you get the August issue, Mom?"

"Yes. I have it right here in front of me."

"Good. See if page fifty-five is in it."

"Just a minute."

He waited a few seconds, his heart pumping faster than ever.

In a moment her voice was back on the line. "Jim, the page is missing. It was torn out."

Jim could barely restrain himself. It *was* Barry!

"Thanks, Mom!" he cried, thrilled that the mystery was solved. "I love you!"

But suddenly a wave of regret drowned out his feeling of elation. In spite of his desperately wanting to know who was at the bottom of all this horrible business, he had hoped it wasn't Barry. They had been friends so long; what kind of a relationship would they have from now on? The rat, Jim thought. The damn, lousy rat!

"Jim? Are you still there?"

"Yes, Mom," he said, his voice softer. "Thanks, again. See you later."

He hung up and turned to Margo. "She's got the magazine with the page torn out of it," he said gravely.

"Hey! At last we're cooking!" she exclaimed, then frowned. "What's the matter? You've solved the case. Aren't you happy it's over?"

He took a deep breath and let it out heavily. "Barry. I would never have believed it."

A bell rang. Their lunchtime was over.

They went to their lockers and then to their respective classes. Jim, heading for Math 10, wished he had the nerve to skip it. Barry was in the class, too. Barry. Oh, man. *We were good friends. At least, I thought we were. Can't a guy trust his own friends anymore?*

He entered the room and saw Barry already in his seat.

"Hi, Jim," Barry greeted him.

Jim ignored him. He felt cold, bitter all of a sudden.

A hand tapped him on the shoulder. "Hey, man, what's up? Aren't you talking?"

Jim looked around. Barry was standing beside him, gazing at him bewilderedly.

"What?"

Barry smiled, put a hand on Jim's shoulder, and shook him. "Are you all right? You look as if you're on a trip!"

Jim stared at him — stared deep into those mild, friendly eyes. Just as he thought. Barry could not have done those terrible things. No guilty person could look into his eyes like that and say what Barry had said.

That left only one other person.

"I should have known," Jim told himself silently. "Darn it all, I should have known."

There was good news when Jim got home that afternoon. The bright, happy glow on his father's face was all he needed to know what had happened.

"You got a job, Dad!"

"Right!"

"Where?"

"At Casey's Company."

"Great!"

He didn't tell his father, nor anyone else in the family, about his own quiet victory. He would wait till later, when he was sure the door was closed on it for good.

* * *

The game with the Floralview Bucs got underway as scheduled that night. It was a hot, muggy evening — better weather for baseball than football.

Jim, standing in front of the Rams' bench, watched the two teams line up for the opening kickoff. He looked at the green-uniformed Bucs, whose front line looked to average three or four pounds heavier per man than the Rams'.

Floralview had a 2–0 record. They had blasted the Riverside Bulldogs last week, 40–7, but had just managed to squeak past the Coral Town Indians the week before, 14–13. The sportswriter for the *Port Lee Daily* gave the Bucs a seven-point edge to win the game. The *Nuggets'* sportswriter-photographer, Jerry Watkins, gave the Rams a six-point edge.

The whistle blew. The Bucs kickoff man raised his hand. Then, on signal, the two lines sprang ahead. *BOOM!* Toe connected with ball, and like a shot the football left the tee and sailed end over end through the air deep into Rams territory.

Tony Nichols, standing on his ten-yard line, caught the ball against his stomach, and rushed up to the twenty-two where he was smeared.

"Well! He finally made it," a strong voice said at his side.

Jim looked at Coach Butler standing beside him. Then he saw that the coach wasn't referring to Tony, but to someone who had just come into the football stadium, Jerry Watkins. The school's sportswriter-photographer, his camera paraphernalia hanging by a strap around his neck, was jogging in.

Jim felt a chill ripple along his spine. He hadn't minded it a bit when the coach had told him he was starting Barry at tight end. He had his mind full of a problem, and until he had the problem cleared away he knew he wasn't worth his salt in the game. He had hoped it would have been taken care of by now, so he would have been able to start. But the source of his problem had just made his appearance.

Jim took a deep breath and exhaled it as he stepped back and started to walk behind his teammates toward Jerry. He had it all arranged what he was going to say to Jerry. He didn't give a darn what Jerry did after that. Jerry might deny every word he said at first. But the minute Jim told him that he had proof — that he had his father's magazine out of which Jerry had torn the page he had mailed to Jim — his goose was cooked. He could not deny then that he was the guy who had made those malicious phone calls, pinned the picture of a convict on the wall of Jim's father's garage, and planted Pat Simmons's drawing pencil on the ground near it to cast the blame on Pat.

The Rams' cheerleaders were chanting:

We've got the coach!
We've got the team!
We've got the pep!
We've got the steam!
Coach! Team! Pep! Steam!
Fight, Rams! Fight!

Jim caught Margo looking at him. She had her hair up in a ponytail. She looked pretty neat in her short pleated maroon skirt, he thought.

She waved to him. He moved his head in a subtle gesture, then said silently, hoping she could read his lips: "Look who's coming!"

She turned. She saw. Then she came running toward him, her face filled with concern.

"I didn't think he'd show up!" she whispered tensely.

He frowned. "Why not?"

She looked at him contritely. "I've already told him, Jim."

CHAPTER • 14

"WHY," HE ASKED. "Why did *you* tell him?"

He had wanted to confront the rat himself. Why did she have to spoil it for him?

"Because I had to know why he did it," she answered. A warm wind blew a strand of her hair across her face. She brushed it back. "Jim, he blamed it on you. He said that if it weren't for that motorbike accident, he would be playing football today, instead of writing about it."

Jim's belly tightened into a knot. "I guess it's not so hard to believe."

"That he blamed you, you mean?"

"Yes. I suppose what happened was my fault, but my bike skidded." He remembered the accident vividly now. He had tried to blot it out of his memory ever since the day it had happened. "It was two years ago," he explained. "We were racing the Winternationals in Tallahassee. Jerry and I were coming around a sharp turn. I was on the inside. I struck a bump, and my front wheel twisted. My bike skidded and rammed into Jerry's. He lost control, ran into a guardrail, and injured his knee."

"He said he was laid up in the hospital for three weeks," Margo said.

"Yes. I went to see him every day. He was bitter about it. But I thought he got over it."

The girls started another cheer.

"I've got to go," said Margo. "See you later."

Jim glanced past her as she dashed off to join the other cheerleaders. Jerry was approaching. He had slowed his pace now to a walk.

Jim glared at him, then turned and started back to the spot he had vacated. He glanced toward the field and stood still as he saw Barry running down to the right flat. A Floralview Buc was about two yards behind him, closing the gap rapidly.

Jim saw the pass floating high through the air. It was coming down in front of Barry. Barry reached for it, got both hands on it, and started to fumble it. For an instant Jim wished he would drop it, to ensure his own starting place on the team. But Barry grabbed the ball before it dropped and pulled it safely to him, stumbling as he did so. He fell, and skidded out of bounds. But he held on to the ball.

A roar rose from the Rams' fans, and Jim found himself cheering, too.

"That-a-go, Barry!" he yelled. "That-a-go, ol' buddy!"

It was a good catch. It was a thrilling catch. Barry's determination to gain a spot on the starting lineup was clearly indicated in that tough play.

Good for him, Jim thought. But Barry's developing into a better player made him realize that he had to get back into the swing himself, or Barry would take over his starting spot as tight end.

"Jim."

He turned. Jerry was beside him, pale, a grieved look on his face.

"I'm quitting my job as sportswriter and photographer," Jerry said nervously.

Jim studied his face. Jerry was sweating profusely. He met Jim's eyes one moment and glanced away the next.

"Jerry, I never realized you wanted to play football so badly that you blamed me for what happened," said Jim.

"I didn't think you did. That's why I" — Jerry coughed — "That's why I did what I did." His eyes blinked. "I just wanted to make one phone call, that was all. I never figured on making more, and doing those other things. But, once I got going, I couldn't stop. I'm sorry."

"Yeah. I hope you're satisfied, because you made it rough for me — and my family — for a while," Jim said. "It wasn't my fault about that accident, but it was pretty rotten what you did."

Jerry's eyes blurred. "I know. I'm sorry. I'm really —"

"Jim Cort!" Coach Butler called. "Get in there! Take Barry's place! Move!"

Jim put on his helmet and buckled the strap.

"Step on it, will you?" the coach snapped.

Jim shot another glance at Jerry, then dashed out to the field. Barry saw him and came running in, one side of his uniform smeared with dirt.

"Nice catch, Barry," Jim said.

"Thanks."

Jim joined the huddle. Chuck looked at him and grinned. "Did you see that catch Barry made? You'll have to get back with it, Jim, or good ol' Barry will be playing more than you will."

Jim smiled. "Anything wrong with having two good tight ends on the right side?" he asked.

"Wow! Listen to Mr. Modest!" Pat Simmons declared. "You're pretty sure of yourself, aren't you?"

Jim shrugged. "Well, I don't mean to sound that way. But I am more now than I have been. And I'm not taking anything away from Barry, either. I'm glad he's coming along so great."

"Okay," said Chuck. "Enough of this yakking or they'll jab us with a five-yard penalty. Forty-three draw."

They broke out of the huddle and went to the line of scrimmage, and Chuck started calling signals. At the snap, Chuck handed the ball off to

Mark, and the fullback plowed through left tackle for a four-yard gain.

The ball was on the Bucs' thirty-three-yard line now. It was second and six.

Chuck glanced at Jim. "Feel like a long bomb, friend?"

"Put it there and I'll catch it," said Jim confidently.

"Okay. Here's your chance to put your money where your mouth is. Forty-nine fly. On three."

On the snap, Chuck faked a handoff to Mark, then faded back and got set for a pass, while Jim broke from his guard and sprinted across the field in a scissor pattern. Down near the ten-yard line he saw himself clear and looked over his shoulder for the pass from Chuck. The ball was coming, a slightly wobbling spiral heading toward the end zone.

It looked as if it were going too far, and Jim accelerated his speed. As the ball came spiraling down he reached out for it, caught it in the palms of his hands, and drew it to him.

Touchdown!

"Hey," exclaimed Chuck, meeting him near the goalposts, "you look like the ol' Jim Cort I used to know!"

"I feel like him, too," Jim beamed.

Mark made the point after good, and the Rams led, 7–0.

They picked up two more touchdowns in the

second quarter to the Bucs' one, and led at the half, 21–7.

During halftime, while the Port Lee High School Band played and marched through a series of eye-catching drills, Jim rested in the locker room with the other members of the Rams. Coach Butler pointed out a couple of mistakes the defense had made that resulted in the Bucs' getting their touchdown. One was Fred Yates's missing a tackle at left end, the other was Chick's running into two of his own men on his way to chase down a Bucs ballcarrier.

"Perfect we can't be," said the coach. "Just work at it, that's all I ask."

Barry, playing again in Jim's place during the third quarter, caught two short passes and was instrumental in the Rams' fourth touchdown. Mark missed the point-after kick, leaving the score 27–7.

Jim saw Jerry moving behind the sideline taking pictures: of Chuck throwing a pass, Barry pulling down a pass, Steve and Pat on a red-dog play, Scott tackling the Bucs' quarterback. You'd never know this was his last assignment. He did his job with enthusiasm. Dedication.

He loved it. You could see he loved it.

The Bucs scored another touchdown in the fourth quarter and got their point after, too.

The game ended with the Rams winning it, 27–14.

Cheers echoed and reechoed through the stadium as fans scrambled down the steps and came to praise their heroes. Jim saw his mother and father and Peg coming toward him, their faces wreathed with happy, proud smiles. But he was looking for someone himself. He was looking for Jerry Watkins.

"Good game, son!" his father declared. "You looked the best since —"

"Just a minute, Dad," Jim interrupted. "I want to see someone, then I'll be right back!"

He turned and almost bumped into Margo.

"Hi!" she said.

"Hi. I'm looking for Jer —" he started to say, and suddenly saw the object of his search walking hastily toward the exit with the crowd. "Jerry!"

Jerry stopped, looked back, and saw him. Jim ran to him, Margo at his heels.

"Jerry — don't."

Jerry stared at him. "What?"

Jim inhaled deeply, exhaled. He felt Margo's small hand slide into his, felt her fingers grip his.

"Stay on as the school's sportswriter and photographer," Jim said tensely.

Jerry frowned. "You mean that you . . . ?"

Jim nodded. "Yeah, I guess that's what I mean."

He didn't wait for Jerry to answer. He turned away and pulled Margo after him. "Come on," he said. "My parents and sister are somewhere in that crowd, waiting for us."

"Jim, you're crazy!" Margo shouted at him. "You know that? You're absolutely crazy!"

"Maybe I am," Jim replied. "What would you have done?"

She stared wonderingly at him. "I don't know."

How many of these Matt Christopher sports classics have you read?

- ❏ Baseball Pals
- ❏ The Basket Counts
- ❏ Catch That Pass!
- ❏ Catcher with a Glass Arm
- ❏ Challenge at Second Base
- ❏ The Counterfeit Tackle
- ❏ The Diamond Champs
- ❏ Dirt Bike Racer
- ❏ Dirt Bike Runaway
- ❏ Face-Off
- ❏ Football Fugitive
- ❏ The Fox Steals Home
- ❏ The Great Quarterback Switch
- ❏ Hard Drive to Short
- ❏ The Hockey Machine
- ❏ Ice Magic
- ❏ Johnny Long Legs
- ❏ The Kid Who Only Hit Homers

- ❏ Little Lefty
- ❏ Long Shot for Paul
- ❏ Long Stretch at First Base
- ❏ Look Who's Playing First Base
- ❏ Miracle at the Plate
- ❏ No Arm in Left Field
- ❏ Red-Hot Hightops
- ❏ Run, Billy, Run
- ❏ Shortstop from Tokyo
- ❏ Soccer Halfback
- ❏ The Submarine Pitch
- ❏ Tackle Without a Team
- ❏ Tight End
- ❏ Too Hot to Handle
- ❏ Touchdown for Tommy
- ❏ Tough to Tackle
- ❏ Wingman on Ice
- ❏ The Year Mom Won the Pennant

All available in paperback from Little, Brown and Company

Join the Matt Christopher Fan Club!

To become an official member of the Matt Christopher Fan Club,
send a self-addressed, stamped envelope (10 x 13, 3 oz. of postage) to:

Matt Christopher Fan Club
34 Beacon Street
Boston, MA 02108